The Vandal

by

Tom Molloy

THE PERMANENT PRESS

Sag Harbor, New York 11963

Library of Congress Number: 89-62513
International Standard Book Number: 0-932966-98-5

Manufactured in the United States of America

THE PERMANENT PRESS
Noyac Road
Sag Harbor, NY 11963

For Rita

I'd like to thank the following people for their friendship and their support of my writing efforts: Jack Zambella, John Volk, Bill Harrington, Jim Gearing, Tim Heider, Toni Johnson, Leni Greason, Frank McCarthy, Dennis Campbell, Jack Warner, Martha Birnbaum, the Molloys, the Doucettes, the O'Briens, the Morrells, and the late Jack Lynch, soldier and scholar.

I have always been a student of sleeping women. A woman naked and unknowing, drawing breaths and exhaling so that the embracing sheet ripples and folds with her breathing, creates within me the hard kernel of knowledge that what I do is correct.

The woman I gazed down at, the woman I was about to leave, was pregnant. She was in that early part of pregnancy that is soft and unfocused, like the false winter dawn moving along the eastern sky beyond the bedroom walls surrounding her. It was coincidence that each of the two times I had left this woman, my wife, she has been pregnant.

I moved through the house silently, peeking in at our four-year-old son, checking locks, the stove, the thermostat. I unfolded the wrappings of my instruments and found that they were just as I had left them; in perfect working order. Without leaving a note, I let myself out.

As I walked, I recalled the night a few months after our marriage when something awakened me to the still house and the white quarter-moon beyond iced windows.

Realizing my wife was not asleep beside me, I raised myself on one elbow and could see her in the far corner of the room, wrapped in an afghan. She was seated in a chair.

When she spoke her silhouette remained still, causing her voice to be very strong in the darkness.

"You had your DMZ dream again."

I didn't remember the dream and thought it had stopped months earlier.

"It was only a dream."

"You have it every night. That means your soul is trying to speak to you."

I got out of the bed and stood by the window, looking out at the fields and the ebony border of the woods. I turned, but from where I stood she was invisible. When she spoke her voice was very gentle.

"You're going to leave me."

"Don't be silly," I told her.

I could see her sharp movement in the chair before her words spilled out.

"Why is it every time a woman knows something a man doesn't, it's silly, but every time a man knows something a woman doesn't, it's common sense?"

Beyond the windows all was still when I spoke.

"I'm not going to leave you."

"You are. I know you love me, and I know you're going to leave."

I hoped for the movement of an animal to break the stillness of the field and its wooded boundary, but no creature ventured forth. Hunter and hunted had business elsewhere tonight. My wife spoke again.

"You can beat bad dreams if you face them head-on."

A breeze from the northeast rattled the windows and caused the chimney flue to issue a metallic yawn. Across the field the tops of pine trees waved at the sky like seagrass in the current of a shallow coastal inlet.

She said, "Don't worry about me if you go. As long as I know you're coming back, I'll be all right. When it's time, just go. No explanations, no excuses. That way I'll know you're coming back and it will be OK."

The wind had passed, and the tops of the pine trees again pointed straight at the moon when she spoke.

"Promise?"

"I promise."

"Cross your heart?"

"Cross my heart."

She came from the darkness and took my hand in hers. Holding the index finger of my right hand, she traced a cross on the left side of my chest and spoke a single word.

"Done."

As it will on very cold days, the snow crunched audibly beneath my boots and I found a cadence between that sound and the puffs of vapor that marked my breathing. I crossed one field, then another, where with a low grunt I went over a thick stone wall built by a long-dead Yankee.

Past the wall I turned parallel to the Kennebunk River, watching the water rush past black and menacing against the clear white snowy banks, gathering speed for its imminent demise in the Atlantic.

Moving on, tripping once on the solid crust of the snow, I could hear an occasional vehicle on Route 1 which runs north-south through the center of Kennebunk. My plan was to reach that road, then hitchhike one hundred miles south to Boston. I hoped I would not run into anyone who knew me, for there were many such people about. I had for some time been a volunteer fireman in Kennebunk. My wife and I had run an arts and crafts shop in town for several years. I have a keen talent for baking and have taught courses in the evening at the local high school.

A number of women taking the courses have, at certain times, offered themselves and their love. But I have, so far at least, always been loyal to my wife, and for that these women have loved me all the more.

Near the town I pushed through a deep dirty snow bank that marked the edge of the road, and I quickened my gait on the shallow snow that carpeted the unseen asphalt. Clipped to my jeans at the hip was a walkman; and in the bag along with my instruments were tapes by Laurie Anderson, Philip

Glass, and George Winston. The walkman had a fine feel to it, and as I walked it pressed against my hip with the snug reassurance of a weapon.

The morning light was spreading over the land in tangible bursts, and it was early dawn when I reached town.

There, along the empty border of Route 1, at the gas station adjacent to the Kennebunk Inn, I let myself in to the station's men's room. My breath was visible in the tiny, unheated room.

The instruments are wrapped in a length of lavender felt, and each is encased in a small leather pouch, the felt and leather being sewn together.

All of these tools were made in the 1800's. The years of care and use have made them almost perfect for the task at hand.

At the bottom of the small knapsack I carry are: an India oilstone, an India gouge slip, pike oil, and a leather strop, all used to keep the instruments well sharpened. The instruments consist of three small rifflers, a small carver's mallet, two straight gauges, two curved gauges, one straight chisel, one curved chisel and a screwdriver. The handle of each is made of hickory. All of them are quite small and fit easily in a man's palm.

In my shirt pocket is a ballpoint pen carved from walnut by a craftsman who lives with blonde twins on a dirt road in Starks, Maine.

As I felt inside the bag, I watched myself in the mirror, where steady puffs of vapor told me my breathing, and things overall, were under control. I chose the proper instrument, and my hand moved along the clean white space between the porcelain and the reflecting glass forming the words:

BEWARE LOVE

I found the letters to be nicely formed with a slight hint of a swirl beneath the first word.

I walked briskly across Route 1 to wait amid the still air and the lovely odor of a woodstove that drifted invisibly amid barren maple branches to rest on the town center.

Like a commuter waiting for his train, I peered down the narrow white thread of the road and waited for a passing car or truck. The scrawled letters on the cold wall had released a deep tension within me, and I felt my whole being relax. Now I was free to travel on to Boston and meet Puma.

I had met Puma only twice in my life, but it was as if he was always there. I could talk to Puma in my mind. Having written to him about my planned journey and its purpose, I had arranged to meet him this day in Boston.

I felt my work would be better focused during this trip if I steeped myself in certain discarded traditions. So I had chosen to remain both incommunicado and celibate.

Yet as I stood, the presence of the sun touched off within me a growing sensual awareness. The thought of sex made me shiver beneath my light, correctly layered clothing.

The road ahead remained a motionless straight white line that held the sunlight. Nearby, lights still lit against the fading darkness, was a small coffee shop. It was newly opened, and I didn't know the woman moving behind the counter. Because of the ice on the plate glass windows, her lower body was a white-uniformed blur, but her shoulders and face were clearly visible. We exchanged a glance. She smiled. I watched the thin empty road.

The hour at which the shop opened for business had not yet arrived, and the full light of day was nearly at hand.

I shifted my weight, the vapor of breath seeming thicker now, and the white uniform moved within its ice-coated frame.

Removing one glove, I tapped on the glass door just above the burnt orange sign that told of the store's hours. She came to the door smiling but shaking her head no. Pointing at the sign she mouthed the opening hour. I removed my cap and waited. She opened the door and the wonderful fragrance of baking dough and ground coffee surrounded me.

When she closed the door a tiny bell chimed, joining the metallic sound as her fingers worked the lock shut, and the burnt orange sign tugged at its string, chafing the worn wooden door.

She said she had seen me around town and decided to let me in because I looked so cold all alone out there. She said the boss would kill her if he knew; she said there was coffee in the back room.

In her late 20's, she had hair of a beautiful light auburn texture touched throughout with the color of honey.

She poured my coffee into a paper cup and stirred the liquid with a metal spoon. I sat on a folding chair as she pulled herself up to sit on a long wooden table opposite me. From a sitting position she added cream and then sugar, spilling some of the white granules on the smooth wood, on the white cloth of her uniform, and the soft curve of her thigh.

She lifted her gaze from the sugar to me and said, "Oops."

The uniform had wide white buttons down the front and she undid three of them as she crossed her legs so that some of the sugar spilled off her thigh and her panties displayed their robin's egg blue.

I stared and she said,

"Do you like sugar? I like it. I like to lick it."

To have her in my arms, to taste the white powder and the salty musk of her skin, to press my mouth to the soft promise of her pubic hair, to feel her tongue on mine, to have her in secret rooms like magic visits to youth's summer night.

When I shook my head no her puzzlement turned to a pout, then a gentle smile and she said, "OK."

We shared a doughnut filled with raspberry, and the paper cups became malleable from the embrace of the hot liquid. Her smile was but an antecedent to the deep embrace of her laughter which came easily when I told her anecdotes about a city boy who moved to the country. I told her I could fall in love with her today except for previous commitments, and her laughter came again.

As I stood outside again, an olive green van grew larger on the road, slowed, and its right amber blinker came to life. The woman and I exchanged a glance. The warmth of her hand created a clear blue hole in the ice on the window. As she moved behind the counter the hole made her seem disjointed. The driver asked how far I was going. I told him Boston.

Chill and airy inside, with a set of tools lying like sleeping children beneath a blanket, the van accelerated until a rooster tail of snow chased us along the road. The driver spoke of his home in Nova Scotia, of his father, his uncle, and the woman he loved back there.

He talked about the whales in the Bay of Fundy and the awesome tides and terrible whirlpools that swept the bay. His words made me more comfortable, and I stretched in the seat, feeling the glass-filtered sun on my face.

As we spun clockwise around the huge traffic circle in Portsmouth, New Hampshire, then veered south, I told him of a terrible storm on the Nantucket Shoals when I'd gone lobstering four years earlier. An unpredicted storm had caught the fleet unawares because a government weather buoy failed.

We had spent two days and two nights in the little wheelhouse, hearing frantic cries for help on the static-filled radio, slamming against the walls, the floor, the berserk wheel, and each other, transfixed by the great gray parade of death all around us. As he checked the rear view mirror, the driver asked,

"What did you talk about?"

The memory of it made me slightly dizzy.

"We never spoke."

He nodded as though passing a familiar friend, and leaned closer to the steering wheel, staring straight down the empty asphalt.

"Ain't that the truth," he said.

Those were the last words either of us spoke until we bid good-bye before the great concrete mass of South Station in Boston.

In the city the air was about ten degrees warmer than it had been in Maine. But the temperature again plunged as I descended the stairs to the subway. Below, the walls of the frigid corridors were covered with plywood, and the plywood was smeared with graffiti, the spray-painted icons of America's underclass.

Looking at it was like peering into the mind of a schizophrenic; chilling, dizzying, disjointed, and possessing the promise that enough exposure would lead to a closing of all escape routes.

The train rolled south past inbound trains disgorging their passengers onto the filthy platforms of the oldest subway in the world. The black, white, and brown faces blurred and spun, mixing together as my near-empty car fled each station.

The stop where I disembarked was called Columbia, and it was above ground. The ancient steel partitions between the tracks seemed to echo the cold and I turned my collar up as I trotted down the stairs. I learned to love walking in the army, and was eager for the miles that led to Puma.

Of course, Americans are afraid to walk. They think they will be robbed or raped or killed. Most afraid are white Americans, who fear they will be killed by black Americans. It's the first thing they think of if their cars break down.

This is one of the basic facts about this country. White Americans are terrified of black Americans. So I walked the near empty sidewalks as cars poured past and I kicked the shallow snow of the city.

I saw him from a great distance, distinctive even from there in his camel hair coat that clearly defined the powerful lines of his body.

Puma maintained a persona that transcended many lines of social strata. He was a man who without moving, without so much as blinking, could cross the line from benign intellectual to truculent nocturnal entity.

Now on the tip of the urban peninsula called Castle Island, he stood with his back to me as he stared past the airport, the harbor islands, and far out to sea.

Its metallic presence made closer by the chill air, a 747 clawed at the sky over Logan Airport, breached the shoreline and passed overhead, its roar wafting behind like a lingering scent.

The plane was a dot, the sound gone distant, when Puma turned his gaze toward the curving, wavering, vanishing speck of the airplane. As he had the first time I met him, he offered a poem.

"The spirit is too weak; mortality weighs
Heavily on me like unwilling sleep

And each imagined pinnacle and steep
Of God-like hardship tells me I must die,
Like a sick eagle looking towards the sky."

The land and the islands lay still, as did the ocean beneath the solid pale blue sky. Puma turned, his ebony skin coming back to reveal his fine wide smile. As we shook hands, he spoke.

"Poems still make you depressed?"

"Yeah."

His laughter was soft, deep, and answered by a lone gull riding the air, shifting its gaze left and right, seeming to suck in the fecund breeze. Puma continued.

"Museums still give you migraines?"

"Yes."

His laughter boomed outward so that the little knots of people scattered about in the chill turned to see, as over the water the gull complained, seeming to call for silence. Puma took a small step closer, his eyes looking hard into mine.

"Think you're ready?"

"Yes."

"And your wife?"

"She understands."

"And your son?"

"He's my son."

Across the water, jet engines loosed a guttural roar as they were reversed to stop a plane moments after touchdown. Puma spoke above the noise.

He said we were in an age of decadence; he said before there was light there was order. Of course, the center could not hold, it was never meant to. We, he added were as matter to space and, he intimated by his gaze, that I was to provide the formula.

"One atom per 1000 litres." I replied.

Telling me of fine ways to travel and warm places to sleep, Puma probed my sense of direction.

Our society was like an army turning a retreat into a rout, Puma continued. In a rout, panicky soldiers feed on one another's fears, running from imaginary noises and shadows. Americans were in a blind stampede from the cities and before too long they'd be running from the suburbs too, running from people they'd never talked to or seen, let alone listened to.

Puma said it was like the Battle of Bull Run when the retreating Yankees would raise the cry, "Black Horse Cavalry" and run in blind fear for the rear. But there was no such thing as Black Horse Cavalry in the Confederate Army. We need to stop, think, and hold our ground.

I told him that I had come to believe that a proper course of action would be an expression of one's belief within a framework of isolation and celibacy; isolation to give a sharper focus to the message and celibacy to maintain a necessary distance, because much of the silliness released in the '60's had eradicated the necessary distance.

Behind Puma, I could see a grounded jet turning sharply, the pilot working the flaps before trying for the air above. Puma spoke.

"But what we do matters."

The white strobe lights of the plane flashed in the harsh sun.

"We don't know what seed is sown."

The plane began moving, a silver presence fleeing its twisting brown exhaust. I felt my heart join the pilot's in its increasing beat. The nose of the plane snapped up, the fuselage lifted gently and carried over the water, over us, and southward over the library of the slain president.

As it passed from sight, Puma queried, "And who will hold sway in the Fulda Gap? Americans with the social and historical perspective of parakeets? Or Russian Comrades lusting after rock music and blue jeans?"

It was a rhetorical question. He knew I took pride in my military service. Although very young when the Korean War officially ended, I was actually a combat veteran of it. I'd been stationed on the Korean DMZ when the nation's eyes were fixed on Viet Nam. We killed and were killed in our forgotten wasteland because of cease-fire violations, the bastard children of feints and intrigue in far away capitals.

The breeze stopped, as off to the northeast I could see a contrail and a silver speck miles high seeming almost to stand still as it strained against the jet stream.

"Where will you be?" he asked.

"Here. Right here in the city. I know it well."

I'd been born in Boston, to parents who died young, weeks apart.

"And for money?"

I reminded him I had a license to drive large trucks. The vagaries of my vocation made tangible labor essential for me. I'd been following the want ads for weeks. I would get a job delivering office supplies and office furniture. I would be in and out of many stores, warehouses, and offices, I would be in an ideal position.

On the water a barge long and low hove into view, attended by two anxious tugs. Like dancers cheek to cheek, they hurried the barge up the channel that forked into East Boston and Chelsea. Puma extended his hand and I grasped it.

"Will you be in the city?" I asked.

He shook his head no.

"I'm involved in a complex project."

As we parted I wanted to ask about the project, but as with so much else about Puma, his reticence seemed correct and proper.

He turned and was quickly gone. I walked rapidly past the L Street Bathhouse, where my father suffered his fatal heart attack at the age of thirty-nine. I went on, beneath the expressway, and watched the faces turn from Irish to brown to black and then to Chinese.

Above a dry cleaners and a small restaurant I rented a room with two bay windows. Through one was a red brick courtyard and through the other I could see the high buildings of downtown. It felt good to be in the city as I lay on the bed holding a newspaper above me with both arms.

There could be no communication with my wife. No phone calls, no letters, no hidden messages among the classifieds.

The sink was made of old porcelain, and it rested on three wide white chipped legs. I undressed at the sink, then washed, careful to get the newspaper ink off my hands and the grime off my face.

Drying my hands carefully, I switched off the lights and parted the drapes, letting in the panorama of Boston.

Like so many American cities by night, Boston seemed like some vast shimmering organism, quivering in contemplation of itself.

Few things are as beautiful as an American city in the dark. Boston, lying between the bracing grip of the Atlantic and the curving, slothful embrace of the Charles River, wore its age like a grande dame her jewels.

In the darkness of the street, the glow of a single cigarette floated in a doorway. Every few seconds the tiny red orb leapt upward as the unseen smoker sucked on the tobacco.

Suddenly the cigarette arced outward and came down in the middle of the roadway, showering sparks.

For a long time nothing moved on the street and no sounds came from the city beyond. At length, a dog came along one side of the street, about halfway between the row of parked cars and the middle of the road. The animal moved at a trot, turning its head to the cigarette like a tour bus passenger to a passing cathedral.

Pulling the curtain shut, I walked to the bed, from where I watched the pattern of light shift on the ceiling. Drifting to sleep, at that point where the subconscious speaks to the mind, I realized that I had not brought a weapon with me. Weapons, when hidden, like secret achievements, bring a certain serenity, a calmness, which makes violence less likely. Reaching with my left arm, my fingertips could just touch the bag on the floor that held the instruments. With that compass, I drifted off in the darkness.

In the morning I rode a bus the short distance to the trucking firm that was looking for workers. The wooden building was two stories high, its gray paint peeling off in long curving strips. The structure was set back from the street behind a rutted dirt yard jammed with empty trucks. At odd intervals the gravel was marked with puddles, some of them holding a sheen of gasoline that created pleasant rainbows in the early light.

The door was unlocked and I let myself into the empty, silent room. There were a few red vinyl chairs, bent with use, and around them a number of overflowing ashtrays. I could hear typing from upstairs. Going up the wooden stairs I caught the scent of cigarette smoke.

The typing stopped as I reached the top. A woman in her early thirties was sitting at a desk, a cigarette dangling from her lower lip, both arms resting on an old black typewriter. She was thin, with a firm body, small breasts, a small mouth, and brown straight hair of medium length. When she spoke the cigarette barely moved.

"Don't tell me, ya forgot your bugle."

"Bugle?"

"Yeah, the one ya blow for reveille, the place don't open for two freaken hours."

"Oh."

"Well that's one way to look at it. Coffee?"

"Yeah, please."

She nodded. "It's all there, help yourself."

I opened packets of sugar, packets of powdered cream and mixed instant coffee with the hot water. I sensed her watching before she spoke.

"Don't go gettin' no funny ideas."

"What?"

"Don't play dumb, just 'cause we're alone. Don't try to get cute, I can handle myself."

I stirred the coffee as I turned and answered.

"Don't worry I'm only dangerous when I have my bugle."

She laughed blowing the smoke across the keys of the typewriter.

"Yeah, sure. Have a seat, you here about the ad in the paper?"

"Yes."

"You know the city, you know the streets?"

"Yes I do."

She asked me how to get to Logan Airport if the tunnels were jammed, she asked me how to get from one neighborhood to another in the city, she asked me what streets intersected in Brigham's Circle, and what secondary roads led out of Boston to the south. After I answered she said I was hired.

When I had filled out two forms, she told me a few of the company's general rules and I asked what I should do next.

"Get lost," she said. "We don't open for two freaken hours."

Outside I climbed onto one of the trucks, opened the door and sat behind the wheel checking the instrument panel. I had experience driving 18-wheelers interstate, but these smaller straight-trucks were a real challenge on the streets of a city. Smaller by far than the semi-trailers, they were nonetheless a job moving through the narrow streets jammed with cars at rush hour. And in Boston's narrow maze of roads and alleyways, rush hour was all day, every day.

I walked through the downtown streets as they began to fill with pedestrians coming in from the suburbs. Single-minded people, their combination of drive and American timidity had landed them in that godforsaken place of scalped lawns, unknown neighbors, and an endless chain of giving rides to blank-eyed offspring.

I much preferred the sight and company of city dwellers: their wit, their cynicism, their slouching cosmopolitanism. Among such people I had a quiet breakfast at the Blue Diner. From behind the newspaper I listened to their talk, their news of city neighborhoods, of fist fights in corner bars and how many cops it took to bring a guy down to the station, the knowing whispers of who was taking what down to City Hall, and who could set things straight.

And in Boston, just as in my boyhood there, the talk of men always got back to one subject. Even now in the frozen brief days of December they touched on the subject of baseball, analyzing again strategies used and not used in the past year, and of who would and would not be ready for spring training in two months. Baseball was in this city like the patterns in a woven fabric. The contours of Fenway Park, the sights, sounds, memories, the very smell of the place, dominated Boston in the summer; and even in winter it was always just beneath the surface, ready to be rationed out, offering identity, warmth, and hope through the lengthening grip of the North Atlantic's winter.

After the meal I walked the streets, now brimming with people, men and women grim against the cold wind, young girls firm beneath long coats and flowing scarves, their wardrobes impeccable but for silly running shoes flashing on their feet.

I walked a circuit of Boston Common, up the slight incline of Park Street and past the golden dome of the State House. In the distance, one could see a statue of Washington on horseback, the animal's foot raised to signify that its rider had been wounded.

As I returned the streets were emptying, the sidewalks seeming to grow wider as the pedestrians scurried indoors. Back at the trucking company several men were milling about in a low-hanging haze of cigarette smoke. None of them paid any attention to me as I stood in the middle of the room, watching the woman descend the stairs. She had a cigarette, unlit, hanging at a sharp angle from her lips.

Proffering a pile of papers, she called out numbers; one by one the men came forward and took some of the papers from her. At length I was the only one left, and she said,

"Two-two-five."

She handed me several forms with addresses and items to be delivered. Then she said, "Remember you ain't a name, you're a number, two-two-five."

They had given me a light load because it was my first day and that was fortunate because I lost a few minutes at almost every stop searching for the right street number, and scanning building directories for the correct office.

By lunchtime I was parked off of Summer Street, an area of wide cobblestoned streets, rundown warehouses, and abandoned railroad tracks. The air was fragrant with the smell of the ocean. Finishing a sandwich, I checked in with the dispatcher and found she knew my voice.

"How ya doin', two-two-five?"

I told her I was fine and asked if she had a number too.

"I'm Frances Lawless, two-two-five." With that she hung up.

The route took me to the western part of the city, to a Brighton neighborhood where I stopped in a variety store filled with locals, rows of magazines, newspapers, doughnuts, and pots of coffee. Some of the newspapers were from overseas; many of them were the county newspapers of Ireland. I ordered a coffee and stood close by the magazines sampling their covers while a heavyset clerk spoke in a hoarse whisper to a customer.

"Hey the niggers are takin' over, they're everywhere, if the Klan don't stop 'em nobody's gonna stop 'em, then we're all fucked and the Russians'll be here in a week. Ain't no Rambo gonna stop 'em, 'cause that's only movie shit, it's gotta be the Klan or nothin'."

I picked up a magazine about the American Civil War, and asked for a second cup of coffee. "Yes sir, anything else?"

"No, nothing."

"Yes, sir."

I took the coffee with me and dropped the magazine on the front seat. I had a run out to the suburbs where I delivered a swivel chair all wrapped in plastic, and two office dividers, one gray, the other white.

I drove from one suburban town to another, the land, the houses, and the people looking the same, white faces, thin bodies, the men ineffectual, effete, seeming more European than American, and carrying an air of Continental prissiness, like the Paris dandies who look so nice and smell so bad. I wondered if their bloodless circles, their humorless caste, foretold a new social atrophy coming to the nation.

I swung the vehicle northward onto Route 128, the wide curving highway that ran in a great arc to the west of Boston. With the growing acceleration, the truck filled with the rush of the cold air from without and took on the steady rocking motion of a small boat on a lake.

After leaving a small package with a computer company receptionist, I strolled out the tinted doors and into the building opposite.

Its interior was identical to the one I'd just left but for the fact it faced a different point of the compass. At the building's directory, where people would stop to gaze for the names of companies, or workers would wait for colleagues, I wrote with a tight lettering,

THIRST

I bent close and with a single breath blew at the dry shavings, watching them fall onto the pale blue carpet with its cigarette burns brown and ugly like gypsy moths on a country road.

As I straightened up, I realized a man was standing right behind me. He was white, of medium build and height, and dressed in an expensive three-piece suit, with a too-tight shirt collar. In his late 30's, he was at that point in life where many men compensate diminishing physical strength with sartorial correctness.

The anger on his face turned to disdain, but as I looked into his eyes, uncertainty tinged with fear began to wrap itself around him.

The elevator repeated its task of opening its doors to the empty foyer. The man swallowed once, and the expensive striped shirt seemed to increase its pressure around his neck. I took a small step closer to him and spoke just above a whisper.

"Don't worry, it's only the truth."

He blinked twice, nodded, and walked to the elevator, which as if rehearsed, opened its doors to him. He kept his eyes on the plastic button he had pushed, as the doors closed and the elevator ascended.

I went out an inconspicuous side door and entered my truck. Glancing up at the office building with all the blank rows of tinted windows, I saw its antiseptic American flag dwarfed by a huge aluminum flagpole. There was a good breeze and the flag snapped and twisted, repeatedly clanging a metal pulley in protest. As I started the engine, I knew the well-dressed man would say nothing about our encounter. He'd be unsure of how it would look in his personnel file and probably had not even dared to look at the message.

As the day passed I worked the route back toward the city and at 4:30 made the last delivery. Like flotsam in a sluggish river, I came with the traffic flow back to the yard with its pallets, trucks, and puddles.

After fueling the vehicle, I entered the office. Frances Lawless did not look up from the shipping form she was reading, as she said, "How'd it go, two-two-five?"

"No problems."

"Atta boy, see ya tomorrow."

The winter sky in the west gave forth soft-hued flares of reds, greens, and pinks as the darkness spread on the heavens, bringing fear and magic to the city. The Christmas lights astride the slopes of Boston Common came on, marking the progress of the pedestrians passing before them with twinklings of reds and green.

On the asphalt paths of the Common the darkness came among the insane men and women on the benches, giving them new bursts of energy to shout at the passersby and the joggers, and the energy passed to the teenaged couples so that the boys gave the girls one-armed hugs, lifting them off their feet.

On Tremont Street on the east side of Boston Common I bought three newspapers from a fat, greasy man wrapped in an apron and sweaters and asked him what the news was. He looked around to make sure none of the regular customers was within earshot. Leaning into the air like a runner at second trying to steal the sign, he said,

"Trouble on the horizon."

"How so?"

"Look around."

I did, and he watched me as my gaze came back to him. Then he spoke,

"I been robbed a lot."

He sold three more papers before resuming.

"Know what they want?"

"No, what?"

He shrugged.

"See, that's it, they don't know neither."

I glanced at the front page of one of the papers as he continued, now in a low tone.

"Ya know what they want ya could stop 'em, but hey, if they don't even know . . ." He sold five papers, he told a young woman the time, then he spoke.

"How'd the Market do?"

The wind tugged the pages as I turned them.

"Up 22 on heavy volume."

He nodded, and resumed speaking.

"You remember when you was a kid, paper's be dropped on the corner box, ya could leave your money on top a the box, no locks, no nothin', nobody took the coins neither."

He hefted a bundle and cut the plastic wrapping with a quick thrust.

"Ya knew it belonged to someone else so ya didn't take it. Ya had respect for other people. That's gone, an' it stays gone long enough it ain't ever comin' back. That's entropy, that's the second law of thermodynamics."

Again he told the time to a young woman, then resumed speaking.

"Myself, I think it's the television. I mean them guys on television, they're assholes from the word go. But everyone wants to be like 'em, so everybody wants to be an asshole. Trouble on the horizon, 'cause personally, an' I don't know I ain't ever been there, but I don't think them guys in Mecca watch that much TV. I mean, on TV an' in the movies, they ain't hardly different no more anyway, we're whaling hell outta them terrorists, 'cept in real life they're fucken Uncle Sam five ways to Sunday. Ya ask me, that's the news, an' ya can throw in we got a race war more or less goin' on, an' a lotta ladies wanna cut our balls off, but I ain't readin' it in the papers, if ya get my drift."

I asked him where the smart money was. He replied.

"Fifteen percent in gold, lookin' to thirty, an' Australian real estate, provided it ain't a pig inna poke. Long term ya gotta like the pharmaceuticals and nursing homes but the latter makes me queasy, and don't forget drilling equipment—again of course long term."

A wave of people came out of the subway toward him and I stepped back,

"Thanks, see ya."

"Sure, pal, that's the news. Trouble on the horizon, entropy, an' a long cold winter, ol' wooly caterpillar knows the score, ol' Farmer's Almanac won't steer ya wrong."

In my room, the aroma of steaming food seemed to come out of the walls, massaging the senses till the senses grew almost numb to the cooking. I had disassembled the sagging metal frame of the bed and now lay atop the mattress on the floor. I held the newspaper above me, squinting at the shaded print. Trouble on all the horizons it seemed, local, national, and international. Or so the paper said.

But I knew horror to have a magical quality when mixed with distance. Like the mirrors in a fun house, distance bent and distorted. As the events drifted closer, as the smoke came to the nostrils, as the children played their games in the ruins, as the pretty women swayed, then did the absolutes, the sure clarity of the righteous and the remote dry up and blow away. Every war had its chuckles.

Even now I could recognize a few faces from the morning before, and I remembered my father holding my hand on a Boston street corner explaining that the same people came to the same buildings every day at the same time.

It was really like a small town, he told me. All you have to do is see the pattern, the trend, the connection. He had made me spell out those words, helping me when I got stuck. Pattern, trend, connection. If people, "folks," he always called them, could see that, they'd stop looking at their feet as they walked, he said.

He always had us think of the city as theater, as a comedy show with healthy doses of tragedy thrown in. Dive right in, he'd say, America's the greatest place in the whole world, and we know that, 'cause John Wayne said so. He took me by the hand to hear the winds of Hurricane Carol shrieking through the telephone wires, a bass to my mother's falsetto from the front porch.

When Trigger Burke came to town to kill Specs O'Keefe for ratting on the Brinks Gang, my father sat his five-year-old son on his knee to explain Mister

Burke's arrival. He always called him Mister Burke and would read from the front page of the *Boston Post* all the latest conjectures, hypothesizing, and moral outrage about Mister Burke.

And when Trigger Burke escaped from Charlestown Prison we were there in minutes, amid the sirens and searchlights.

Next day the adults took me onto the back porch, my father always called it the piazza, to tell me my father was dead. I asked did Trigger Burke shoot him, and was secretly disappointed when they said no. But as my father liked to say, that was then and this is now.

Hunger gave a quickness to my steps, the cold a certain perception. On the side of Boylston Street opposite the headquarters of the Boston Police Department, I stopped at the northeast corner of a building.

I was at the edge of an alley that ran for blocks behind the backs of the expensive stores fronting on Boylston Street. Here all the doors were gray. The dumpsters, the color of the doors, lay at odd angles, like landing craft after desperate maneuvers.

I passed several of the doors, then stopped at one adorned with the name of a fashion designer. The brass padlock on the door was worn smooth and pleasant from use. The wind, heralded by gently billowing papers came down the alley. I turned one shoulder into it as I worked, partly shielded by a dumpster.

The message took quite a few minutes, but would

remain on the lock for some time. I was gambling that the owner would not quickly part with such a familiar thing as the smooth lock in the narrow and frightening alley.

The wind lifted dust that came into my eyes and I waited, blinking for relief, the instrument in one hand. Finally, I completed the last letter and moved on.

At each end of the alley people were parading past in ever thicker rows and I worked faster on the next door, which opened to a franchise that sold coffee, soups, and ice cream. The message was nearly complete when a movement behind one of the dumpsters caught my eye. The bum must have been lying there the whole time I worked, but I hadn't seen him. He cursed and lifted himself up on one elbow, the blood from a head wound coming down his forehead and splitting into an inverted V at his nose, then flowing in crimson richness down each cheek.

He blinked, one eye open full, the other slowed by sleep or filth or both.

"Got a buck, buddy?"

Uncurling a dollar from the pocket of my jeans I folded it twice and dropped it onto his lap.

"Butt?"

"Don't smoke."

"Motherfucker, gotta match?"

I pulled out a book of matches as he squinted up at me. Then he pulled out a cigarette, surprisingly white and straight. He held the sleeve of my coat as I held the flame.

"The fuck ya doin'?"

"Working."

Even from a sitting position he swayed, looking at the cigarette as though it had just blossomed from beneath his flesh. He slumped into the cruel concave of the dumpster for support but only banged his head. The pain seemed to give him more life.

"You ain't fucken workin'."

I didn't answer but turned to my carving, looking askance at a white police car nosing into traffic from the station on Berkeley Street. Now his voice was raised.

"Says you ain't doin' no fucken workin'."

He brought his hands up over his head, fending off the metal of the dumpster, and then managed to push himself away from it. He crawled closer, sucking on the cigarette.

Like a man being pummeled by an angry surf he staggered to his feet and slumped against the wall. Butt in his mouth, he waved both hands at unseen demons.

"Stay away from me, I'm tellin' ya, stay the fuck away."

Turning his head to one side he seemed to forget I was present, and he sat down in the doorway, his legs crossed beneath him.

The last letter took shape beneath the instrument as the traffic sounds increased. I worked the shavings out of the newly formed letter and blew once on the words. The bum began to speak.

"Think I don't know? I know plenty. Boss says, 'ya don' like it get off the buildin',' was makin' 22 bucks a hour, 22 a hour, more 'an you'll ever make, so fuck 'em I says, shoulda threw 'em off the fucken buildin', coulda gone worked onna Alaska pipeline, coulda done that, think I don' know that? Fucken country, fucken Viet Nam think I don't know? Fucken cunts, fucken cocksuckin' assholes, niggers shittin' on everybody, even got nigger cops christsake."

A delivery van pulled into the far end of the alley blocking the traffic, making the pedestrians squeeze between it and the white buildings.

"Hey."

He pulled down his zipper and began to fondle himself.

"Ain't doin' no fucken workin'."

His hand moved and stroked as his prick became engorged. He let his head fall back against the gray door, smiling, as his prick stood erect and gray, huge in the pale sun and the furtive footfalls of the office workers, growing even larger with his laughter, his whole arm moving as he thrust his hips outward, laughing, the white semen shooting in uneven spurts onto the dumpster, his pant leg, the hard asphalt, as his arm moved and moved then stopped, though the laughter continued.

"Think I don't know huh? I know plenty mother-fucker, you wait, fucken country, all got their head up their assholes, they'll get theirs. An' I been to Paris too, an London, I know plenty."

He belched, then with both hands he carefully put his prick back into his pants. He used two hands to close his zipper and brushed off his fly. He stood, raising his fists as he swayed, flexing his shoulders like a boxer.

"Let 'em come I'm fucken ready for 'em, ready for all of 'em. Think I'm ascared, I ain't ascared a nobody, spit in their fucken eye's what I says."

He turned and as though walking the slanted deck of a schooner made his way toward the passing line of pedestrians and began to shout at them. Even from this distance you could see them shrink, pretending not to hear as he shouted louder, and his stride became more certain.

By the time he reached the edge of the alley that opened onto Arlington Street, his coat was billowing behind and he strode like Ahab after his whale, the curtain of pedestrians opening and closing around him, the traffic stopping for him as he strode cursing them all, his shadow bouncing on the pale granite walls.

Now I could hear the muffled sound of voices and movement behind this door, so I finished my work. The letters were clear in the sunshine, the words simple:

YOU AND YOURS

At the mouth of the alley a beautiful woman caught my glance and smiled a smile so gentle that it only touched the corners of her mouth, a smile saying, "For you, for you," and faded back into the crowd that flowed and lapped the bottoms of the empty buildings.

The drivers' lounge held a pleasant aroma of discarded pastry tinged with the tart fragrance of spilled beer, the presence of which was enhanced by the smoke of long-extinguished cigarettes. The room lay in chilly darkness, a fuzzy snapshot of careless masculinity.

Above, I heard Frances open a file drawer and take a few steps to her desk. I went up the stairs deliberately so as not to startle her. She had a manila folder close to her chest, looking at it intently, as though it were a menu. She glanced up when I came in the room.

"Two-two-five."

"Hi."

"Hi yourself."

I smiled and she smiled too. I went over to the couch, sat, and stretched, my legs taut, letting the weary stiffness flow from my neck down past my shoulders. It went to my legs and settled there. There is driving and there is driving, and there is driving a truck in Boston on the Friday before Christmas.

With my eyes closed, I felt as though the room was slowly spinning. But that feeling passed, and I opened them as she poured white wine into a plastic glass almost as wide as it was high.

Genuinely thirsty, I nodded my appreciation and took the wine, resting the soft cup bottom on the fingertips and thumb of my right hand. She smiled when I finished, and she refilled the glass. Frances gestured toward the stairs and the lounge below.

"Ya missed the big party."

She was being sarcastic; I could tell she didn't like the drivers, liked them even less when they were full of beer and themselves, chanting the names of streets and intersections like the Sunday pious in prayer.

"Thanks for the wine."

She had poured herself some and raised her glass. I could tell she'd already had quite a bit and now this glass was nearly drained. Returning to her seat she leaned forward, pressing the glass between the heels of her hands, which in turn were squeezed tight by her knees. The plastic bent in silence when she spoke.

"You in trouble?"

"Huh?"

"With the cops like, you runnin' away, you in some kinda trouble?"

"No."

She stared for a few moments, a slight squint touching her features.

"You're different, you ain't like them other guys."

She finished the wine with a single long deep draught, her gaze broken by two quick blinks, then she came off the chair and to my side. Without expression she reached up and took the walkman earphones from my neck and put them on. Adroitly, she flipped the tape to high speed and ran it forward, then back, forward, then back.

Closing her eyes she swayed at the hips, absorbing the sounds through the earphones. Sliding her arms around my neck she spoke only one word. "Dance."

We moved about the warm room, her head turned slightly, her face pressed to my chest, her features content. When she spoke her voice was loud, the way people's voices get when they wear the earphones.

"Men can't hear the music anyway."

Her laugh too was made loud by the earphones, then she swayed and hummed along with the music. Minutes passed, her hands moved from my shoulders, unsnapping two buttons of my shirt. Her lips, wet, soft, reassuring, traced across the coarse hair of my chest. She pulled the earphones back and let them fall to her shoulders where they held her hair like a barrette as she spoke.

"Tell me a secret."

The flavor of the wine mixed with the natural vanilla musk of her skin.

"I can't make love."

Another song came through the earphones like a whispered conversation far down a wood-panelled hall. She ran her tongue along my throat, squeezing the back of my head and breathing through her mouth said,

"Can't or don't want?"

When I did not answer right away she moved back silently, her eyes luminous. Without taking her gaze from mine, her hand moved to my crotch. She squeezed the growing bulge there and I exhaled from the near-overwhelming desire. Now her voice was girlish, playful.

"Can't or don't want?"

We danced between the couch and the metal cabinets. I led her close to the windows where their cold breeze and the heat of the radiator washed over us. She pressed herself very close until I put my hands on her shoulders and she stopped.

Now her eyes quivered in the dim light, reflecting the unmoving objects in the room. In her eyes was the ebony outline of the man before her and the eyes widened very slightly when I spoke.

"Take your clothes off."

She took a quick breath and seemed to quiver from either fear, anticipation, power, submission, or the simple chill of the wide room.

The garments fell in silence between us, her panties on the blouse that lay on her skirt, the bra last of all, seeming too small for the breasts that arched outward, the nipples outlined in the darkness, erect, simple, beautiful.

She began to wrap her arms around herself, but hesitated, then let them fall by her sides. Her gaze came up to me slowly, without a trace of shyness.

Her lips moved very slightly, her throat constricted, but no words came forth. I spoke.

"Lie on the couch."

She did as I told her, and now both her arms came around her body, trying to still the rising goose bumps and her voice was again childlike.

"It's awful cold."

"Be quiet."

I crossed the space between us, then knelt beside the couch. With one hand I touched her foot, squeezing it gently, then ran my finger along her calf, behind her knee, and along the widening inside of her thigh. I brushed her pubic hair with the tips of my fingers, caressed the firm contour of her side, her breasts, the soft lines of her neck.

Still kneeling, I pressed my lips against hers, my arms around her shoulders, lifting them a few inches from the couch, feeling her mouth widen on mine as we drew breath together. I kissed her neck, her hair, and moved my lips across her nipples. Gently, firmly, I pressed the palm of my hand to her crotch, letting one finger slide into the warm moist opening. Eyes closed, her head arched back, she moaned softly as I took her hand in mine and guided it between her legs. She caught the movement of my fingers and rhythmically began to masturbate.

I stood. Her eyes were closed tight as I walked across the room to the chair. Then she swallowed several times, her mouth coming open, her hand moving faster and faster till her palm was sounding against her skin as she arched upward, digging in her heels, thrusting her hips up, drawing in air, moaning and drawing the air in and in till she loosed a long guttural sound, and fell flat, her breathing moving her stomach, her breathing filling the room until the breaths became shallow and far apart.

Now the room seemed warmer, smaller. Lying naked and sure she came back to it, to me, to herself. Her eyes blinked and she touched her throat as though she was very thirsty. I too was thirsty, but it was a thirst from the dizzying warm liquid horniness that filled me, that was backing into my throat, drying my mouth.

Pouring out two fresh glasses of wine, I came beside the woman on the couch, looking askance at her body, like cream in the dim light, beautiful with its dark pubic smudge. I sat on the floor facing away from her, my back against the couch.

"Talk to me," was all she said.

I took a long sip of the wine and wrapped one hand around the bottle that stood on the floor. I tilted my head back so that it rested on the warm, forgiving curve of her rib cage. I took another sip of the wine, feeling the beat of her heart close to my ear.

Then I told her what I was doing. While I talked, the steady red and white streams of automobile lights on the Southeast Expressway thinned until there were growing gaps of darkness on the eight lanes of asphalt.

I paced back and forth in the darkened room,

occasionally glancing up to see the moist white pools of her eyes as they followed my words and footsteps.

At one point she rose on one elbow to listen, drawing her knees closer to her, then running one hand lightly down her thigh, caressing the back of one knee, massaging the flesh there with her thumb and one finger.

"Marx said, 'The capitalists will sell us the rope with which we hang them.'"

I tasted the wine and put down the glass. "It seems to be happening. And it just comes down to selfishness with a healthy dose of cowardice. People don't want to know anything, they want to make money and be left alone. Things start to go downhill in a neighborhood they move to another neighborhood, maybe another state, they don't even consider making a stand. White Americans are afraid of their own cities. Of course they're scared to death of blacks, white men more so than the white women. War goes on in Viet Nam nobody gives a damn. Eighteen years have to go by before they can bring themselves to go to a damn movie about Viet Nam. The Israelis bomb and torpedo one of our ships, machine gun the survivors in lifeboats, nobody says, "Gee that's rude,' nobody says anything, nobody cares. Arabs stick a gas pump up our ass because we support Israel in a war, all people care about is finding the shortest line at the gas station. Inflation goes sky high, people out of work, out on the street, guys lose their jobs, hit the bottle and use the little woman and the kids for punching bags, guys blow their brains out because the Arabs turn off the oil and they lose their jobs, and all anyone can say is, 'Hey where's the gas station with the shortest line?' "

I walked to the window watching the red and green lights of an airliner arcing into the sky over Boston Harbor. I spoke looking through the glass.

"Once in Korea I watched a man kill two innocent people. I actually got a medal for watching him kill them. That night I went to a whorehouse and screwed a little girl who was probably twelve, Christ she could have been ten for that matter. Afterwards something just clicked that maybe I wasn't quite living up to my Ivy League education, and that maybe when I got back to the States, wearing a suit, and having a big desk in a nice office, and kissing the boss's ass, didn't mean diddly. I mean hell, if I'd got the medal for killing those people myself . . . but Christ, all I did was watch."

She stretched on the couch, one hand supporting her head as she listened.

"Two weeks later I went AWOL, holed up in Seoul with two stewardesses, one Japanese, one Australian. Stayed in all day, moved by night. One night I was in a little bar way back in a neighborhood where just Korean workers hung out and this black guy comes in. He's a couple years older than me, built like a bull. Comes right up to me and he says, 'AWOL?' Just like that. And I said 'Yeah.'

"He puts his hand out and says, 'Puma.' "

"Well I'm waiting for the doors to burst open and 15 M.P.'s to beat the hell out of me. I mean who is this guy? I thought he had to be Military Intelligence or F.B.I. hell, maybe he's James Bond doing a minstrel routine, but nothing happened. He was all alone, and he was a civilian.

I spun on the floor so that I was facing her as I continued.

"So we started to talk. This guy's been to 'Nam, now he's in Korea, he's been to Moscow, London, Belfast, Jerusalem, Paris, Manila, Honolulu, New Delhi. To put it briefly he's going around the world. 'Tying the knot,' he called it."

The woman stood, gathering the silk slip around her as she walked. She came over to me and took the glass from my hands, then bent to pour more wine into it. She took a sip of the liquid, handed me the glass and returned to the couch.

I resumed speaking. "I just trusted him, I'm still not sure why, but I just did, like I trust you. I told him about getting a medal for watching a guy shoot two people. I told him about the ten-year-old whore, and about the two stewardesses and our ménage à trois. I told him that I wasn't a coward but that I had not enlisted to watch in silence as innocent unarmed people got murdered, the reward for my silence being a medal, a handshake, and a three-day pass from which I had declined to return.

Outside a car entered the yard, its headlights sweeping the frozen gravel and empty trucks once, then it spun around kicking up pebbles and was gone.

"In brief I told him I was lost, alone, scared, very, very angry, and as confused as I was pissed off. I added that I felt I had failed and disgraced my parents, even though both had been dead for many years."

She turned on one side.

"What did he say?"

"He said a whole lot. He said I should return to my unit and face the consequences of my actions. He said he knew I was considering suicide, which I was, and he said that such a thing would be a terrible waste and a betrayal of purpose. He said I felt lost because my country had lost its way, something, he said, that seems to happen once or twice every century, something, he said, whose measure of depth can be taken by everyday rudeness and selfishness. He said he would contact me again and took my name, rank, serial number, and my address in the States, and he walked out the door."

I got up and sat close to her on the couch as she curled her feet up to make room.

"Next morning I bid adieu to the two flight attendants, walked back to my unit, told my commanding officer I had been Absent Without Leave and got put in a cell. After two days I was taken out of the cell, and told to dig a hole six feet deep and six feet square. When I dug it I was told to fill it in. That was repeated five times, the show losing a little charm with each performance.

Somewhere in the distance fire engines sounded, their cries merging into one and stopping.

"After a number of other punishment details I was returned to my unit. Eight months later I was honorably discharged. I met a girl from Maine, married her and moved to a house in the woods around Kennebunk."

The fire apparatus began the trek back to the station, their bells chiming rhythmically in a two-one-three cadence.

"I'd been married almost a year when Puma came walking up to my front door. My wife happened to be visiting her family at the time.

He really got a chuckle out of my tale of digging holes in Korea, said it no doubt gave me an appreciation of what the poor infiltrators had to go through. After a drink of brandy he'd brought, we went for a walk through the woods and talked.

The woman sat up, folding her hands on her lap and leaning forward.

"He told me he was also a veteran of a forgotten war, the invasion of the Dominican Republic. He was wounded there, knocked off a bridge by a sniper's bullet. He said we were now entering an epoch of ignorance, and America was the center of it. All things being equal, America was the country in which ignorance most translated into danger, a danger that was both foreign and domestic. Finally he said, it all comes down to a willingness to act."

The room was very quiet and past the frosted

windows the cold settled closer to the ground, pressed down by the thickening darkness. I walked to the window and stood with both hands in my pockets.

"That's it, bare bones."

She repeated, "Bare bones."

"Yeah."

She asked me about Puma, his real name, where he was from, where he got his money, where he went to school, if he was married, what he was doing now. I only knew that he had been married at one point and that there was at least one child, and he possessed a rich and subtle appreciation of women.

I knew that he lived simply and resented strongly the modern media image of the American black man which he once described to me as all fists, no brain, jive talk, and sunglasses. Puma hated sunglasses as much as he loved poetry, Mozart, astronomy, and the fiction of Fitzgerald.

I'd heard about how he used to go up to kids who were carrying boom boxes and wearing sunglasses, flip off their glasses and smash the boom box. He'd then slip the kid a pair of crisp new hundred dollar bills and say, "Try thought."

When I told her about that she laughed aloud, then shook her head so that her hair came onto one side, exposing one of her small ears.

When I finished speaking she turned onto her side, took my head in her hands, and kissed me twice on the face. A long liquid hiss came from the radiator as the pipes below clanged like someone banging on a mansion door. That sound made her words seem very soft.

"I was always a lady, always a good girl. I was never a bad girl. They always mixed me up with their smart talk, an' they'd get me confused with it, so I didn't know what was what. But they all wanted the same thing all right, 'cept maybe one, but I never hurt nobody which is more than I got back from them, ever."

Because of the angle she lay at she slurped the wine as she drank.

"An' all that women's lib stuff, hey I'm liberated an' all, but I like havin' doors held open an' all that nice stuff. I wish more of 'em did it, some guys are just so rude, ya know?"

I spoke with the glass in my hand.

"Yeah."

She sniffed and let a small laugh pass her lips.

"No ya don't. They beg an' cry, an' carry on like little kids, little kids I'm tellin' ya, ask anybody. An when ya feel bad an' give 'em what they want you're a whore, an' don't the whole freakin world know 'bout it the next day, ya know?"

I said I thought I did, but she made the same noise as before, but this time it was more of a laugh.

"No ya don't. Once, I did somethin', OK it was stupid, an' I was stupid to do it. It was where I was workin' with this one guy, ya know, out in a car after work one night, an' don't the whole damn world know about it the next day?"

Her fist hit the pillow with a muffled thud, and her voice rose.

"I mean don't just the whole goddamn world gotta know next day, huh?"

Without answering I sipped the wine, noticing how clearly sounds carried in the outside cold. I thought too that the highway looked closer in the cold. There was a rustling behind my head as she pulled on her panties and the blouse.

She bent over so that her hair fell in a bunch and brushed my face, her hand was very cool on my neck.

"I'm yours right now if ya want."

My voice wavered from the want and I had to swallow twice.

"No, it's OK."

"Sure?"

My voice sounded even tighter.

"Yeah sure, it's OK, really."

She was still again but for her fingers that lightly touched my hair. As they moved, I spoke of my wife, of the proper methods for making bread, of how it is no coincidence that it is the bakers who each day greet the dawn. Again the pipes sounded in the walls deep below.

I talked of Korea and the never ending frozen hills of the DMZ we patrolled so many years after the war was supposedly over. I told her of the hate so clear and true along that line that you could taste it on your tongue.

My tale of foreign winters made her chilled, and

she dressed quickly, but my want did not diminish. We agreed I would spend time with her and tell no one. We would come to work at different times, and from her apartment I would come and go as I pleased. So would she. She would have an extra key made, and I would sleep on her couch, or if I preferred in a sleeping bag on the floor.

I would meet her later this evening in a doughnut shop at an intersection close to where the offices gave way to warehouses and they to the docks and the sea. We parted, kissing good-bye like siblings.

I walked blocks before the last remnants of sexual want drained from me. My pace was fast and I trotted across several streets, one hand in a coat pocket, fingers tight against my instruments, for the cold could be hard on them.

At a long row of phones on the street level inside the Greyhound bus terminal I took out one of them. I shivered as I did so, I could feel and smell the cold as it rose from my clothing and skin.

I remembered a night in Korea. They had captured our ship on the high seas, and now on the land, the shells were passing overhead, cold steel orbs tearing the atmosphere like razor blades passing through fine white paper. The infiltrators had gotten behind us, in front of us, among us.

I was crying, the tear and mucous frozen on my face, I was shouting and shooting at shadows, and the shells flew and flew and the evenly spaced automatic rifles sounded correctly. The radio net was a hysterical jumble of southern accents, the ground we lay on hard, cold, and even blacker than the empty Korean sky that mocked us.

The call signs were jumbled, the frequencies were wrong, the units in confusion, the young men counting their time in seconds, when Sergeant Dalton came on the line. Diamond Jim Dalton's Virginia drawl cleared the channels of the terrified cries of all of us, and saved our asses one and all. I traced his words across the face of the wall above the phones.

WHAT THE FUCK? OVER.

Below us on Storrow Drive the cars fled the city four abreast in an unbroken chain of light that changed from white to red beneath the footbridge Puma and I stood upon.

In the distance, the Hatch Shell where the Boston Pops Orchestra played was a rounded cold smudge, and close by it a bronze George Patton prepared to lift field glasses to his eyes.

Puma, his back to me, faced the Hatch Shell, and Patton faced the fleeing motorists so that his ebony figure was sharply etched. Puma hadn't said a word as I told him about Frances, my job, and our new living arrangements.

When I finished speaking he turned to face me, like a spectre among the moving white lights. His words came above the sounds of the automobiles.

"Why now? Next week is Christmas. Why not wait 'til spring? Nice weather, pretty girls in their finery. Lots of people out and about and lots of daylight. The coeds could consider your work as they enjoyed their ice cream cones. Your wife and son wouldn't spend Christmas alone. Neither would you for that matter. What brought you back now?"

I wondered if he could see me clearly against the ebbing tide of red. It had been almost five years since I'd last travelled. I was in my late 20's then, a little thinner, a little quicker, with an anger closer to the surface, but not as focused as now.

For months I had crisscrossed the south in the fecund heat of summer until I left a message on the wall of a bar on the outskirts of Atlanta.

Suddenly surrounded by police officers I was handcuffed and beaten unconscious, awaking with a severe concussion and charges of breaking and entering, resisting arrest, and assaulting a police officer. A charge of possession of burglary tools was dropped.

The beating ended my odyssey in the urban South in which I had travelled unseen and untouched by what lay around me, like a canoeist riding a river's strong current. Indirectly, it set in motion the events that led from the careless freedom of bachelor-hood to the measured steps of marital intimacy.

Having survived shot and shell in the service of my country, I had, like many men before me, returned to these shores with a gentle love for the nation. A love that goes very much unexpressed by men, it is within their chests like the after-glow of fine liquor or the perfumed scent of the lover recently held.

But the beating and the long convalescence that followed gave rise within me to the realization that this special feeling was a one-way street whose direction was reversed only for dead people and the abstraction of a once-a-year holiday. It was like being in love with a woman who's in love with a jerk.

I drew the coat closer to me before speaking and took one hand from a pocket as I pointed at the motorists fleeing with the sun from the city.

"They're running scared, they'll commute two hours each way so they can live in a little white box in the suburbs. There's a very serious shortage of truth around. Worst of all, people in this country are so frightened all the time, but they don't even know what they're afraid of."

Below a horn blared, its pitch falling to a flat monotone as the car raced into the distance. I took a step closer to Puma as the lights cascaded around him. I felt like an actor peering into the footlights.

Puma hunched his shoulders as a police car shot past below, blue lights flashing as it elbowed aside other vehicles. The blue strobes touched the toes of Puma's shoes as he spoke.

"Are you going to tell them what they're afraid of?"

"I'm just trying to tell the truth," I replied.

"So are others," he said.

"Not many," I answered.

"Hundreds," said Puma.

Another police car passed as I spoke. "Hundreds isn't many."

"Hundreds," he said, his voice rising, "have toppled governments and changed the course of life on the planet. Christianity started with twelve, National Socialism with not many more, the American Revolution with only a handful.

The silence between us lengthened as Puma waited for me to speak. Glancing at the night skyline of Boston with its beautiful glass cathedrals of capitalism, I answered him.

"Why now? Because it's the winter solstice, because it's dark and freezing cold. Because the truth needs challenge to be true and what greater challenge is there than America? Because America doesn't care. It would be easier to dodge the secret police with their midnight knock than to try to push off this mush of affluence. They won't even dignify us with their oppression. The truth is beneath their contempt; maybe it was always like this, I don't know. But it's our art, it's what we are. Whether you're on or off, The Journey is always there waiting, The Journey is always true. The phonies climb on with their trends and their social connections, but they never last. The truth isn't packaged in a pretty blue bottle wrapped with a ribbon, but it's a fine gift to give and get and to pass along. It matters. It's energy. No creating, no destroying, only the same simple thing in a different form. So that's why and that's why now."

In the darkness I saw him nod agreement, understanding, acceptance or perhaps a combination of the three. He turned to his left so that he faced the brownstone buildings of the Back Bay when he spoke.

"I'm going to the Pacific Northwest tomorrow. First to Seattle, then to a series of small towns in Oregon. What magnificent trees they have there. They're older than the United States, some older than Columbus."

"You'll be in touch?"

"Eventually."

We shook hands and he walked toward the darkness but halted at the flight of stairs that connected the little bridge to the city and called back to me.

"How many litres?"

"A thousand."

"How many atoms?"

"One."

He descended the metal stairs and was gone.

I went down the opposite stairs, walking over a mile to Charles Circle where an all-night drugstore looked out over a non-stop kaleidoscope of orbiting traffic.

Heading south on Charles Street toward Boston Common, I stopped in front of an expensive boutique. Next door, the window of a travel agency advertised a 60-day tour of the world on a luxury liner. The instrument worked well, and the single word came easily to the cold wood.

SHARE

On the evening of the second day I stayed with her, Frances Jean Lawless lay on her couch watching the smoke of her cigarette redefine itself in the last rays of that day's sun. She had not moved from the couch since I'd left the house almost three hours earlier to jog and swim. Vigorous exercise is an antidote to an unwanted, but common, companion of my vocation. Despair.

I felt splendid from the workout and during my run along the hardened banks of the Charles River I had defined the parameters of several messages. Now while sitting on the floor I massaged the cork of a champagne bottle, till it came free with a sound like stone hitting deep water.

Frances Jean spoke. "The first guy . . ."

Her hand passed through the smoke as though she disagreed with its message and she spoke again as the smoke curled downward.

"The first guy I ever had was real nice. I was only thirteen, and a skinny runty-lookin' kid, ya know?"

I said I did.

"My folks sent me to summer camp for two weeks

'way out in the western part of the state where the mountains are, ya know?"

She waited, then continued.

"One day, oh it was real hot, and even hotter in our bunkhouse. Well anyway I snuck out and went to town to get some cigarettes."

She laughed aloud, blowing fresh smoke into the clouds over her head. Her right arm fell so that her fingertips brushed the rug.

"Can you imagine? I was kinda fresh when I was a kid. 'Bold as brass,' my mother used to say."

She gently sucked on the cigarette, its tip becoming prominent in the fading light. Her lips made a smacking sound before she spoke.

"I was walking back to camp with my pack of Luckies tucked in my little shorts when a big yellow car pulled up with a man driving."

She paused. I poured champagne until it bulged over the edge of the glass, testing the limits of its own elasticity, quivering whitely as it was lifted. She continued her account.

"He asked me if I wanted a ride, and I sure did 'cause it was a long walk. He was dressed real nice, with a suit and a tie, the way I always wished my dad would of dressed, but he never did. He smelled real nice too, with nice cologne, not that Old Spice stuff my dad used to put on every freaken Sunday."

She passed the cigarette from one hand to the other and then back again.

"He turned on the radio and that big yellow car just glided down the road, and he told me what a pretty girl I was which nobody had ever done before."

I traced the lip of the glass with the tip of my index finger, then touched the fingertip to my tongue. She continued to speak.

"He kept talking and we went right past the camp, and he asked if I was hungry and when I said yeah, he stopped at a place and got me a Coke an' fries, and I can remember all the bugs around the big red neon sign. Then we drove away and I remember licken' the ketchup from the fries off my fingers, and how big the dark was all around the lights of the car, and how he made me feel safe, even though he didn't have real big muscles or nothin', and I watched all the dark goin' by, and he told me he knew a real nice place not far away."

The cigarette smoke rose in a straight column, expanding and slowing.

"We came to a pond with the moon real white and real close over the trees and he said, 'get out,' and we did. Then he asked could I swim, so I told him yeah that I'd even got a medal from the Y once, and he just nodded and said, 'Take your clothes off and we'll go for a swim,' so I did like he told me."

She drew again on the cigarette.

"The water was real nice and without sayin' nothing we swam out to a raft in the lake. And right there he pressed me against the raft and I could feel him right inside me and it was wonderful, and he held me real nice and gentle and we floated just on top of the water then he kissed me and kissed me and kissed me and I just went crazy, and he kissed me more and more and it was just the most wonderful thing I ever even imagined."

Her fingers felt for the ashtray on the floor and without looking she crushed the cigarette into the metal. The layer of smoke drifted higher like sea fog waning in the dawn as she spoke again.

"I was like warm but kinda cold at the same time and I had my eyes closed and we floated and floated, my head on his shoulder as he held me up. I could smell his skin and the water, his skin smelled so nice with the water right there, ya know I ain't never smelled nothin' so nice since, not ever, and I ain't just sayin' that neither."

The woman stroked the rug with the back of her fingers, swallowed once and resumed talking.

"Then we came in from the water, and he took his shirt and rubbed me all dry. He was real gentle, he even had me lift each foot so he could dry them too, but all of a sudden I knew I'd never see him again. He didn't say nothin' about it but I knew, and in the car I stared and stared at him, ya know like memorizing his nose, his chin, his eyes, his ear, and his hair, and stuff that ladies notice, then he took me right back to the entrance of the camp and he just kissed me on the cheek and said good-bye, and I watched them red lights of his car go away gettin' smaller and smaller, and that's just like how my heart felt, like it was just gettin' smaller and smaller till it hardly even wasn't there, till it was just so small it couldn't even break, 'cause it was just too small to do even that."

She brought the cigarette up, looked at it, but did not touch her lips to the white paper.

"I used to lie awake in my bunk an' think of him, and I used to sneak out to the front of camp to where there was a big rock, and sit on the rock an' watch the cars come by, and wait for him but he never came. The other kids called me 'Stoney' 'cause I used to sit on the rock, you know? So that was that, and he never came, but I remember that night all right, and I know I'll never forget the way the water and him smelled together, how we floated and floated, and it ain't never been the same since, but I got that inside me, so nobody can take it ever. 'Least I got somethin' special, and no one can take it, not ever."

A minute, then another, then long slow seconds passed. She turned her head toward me, the smoke very close above her.

"Ya know?"

"Yes."

Her hand moved slowly along her stomach and brushed flat a wrinkle in her slip.

"I still love him, I really do."

The smoke began to vanish in the dim air, and with the falling darkness the woman almost disappeared in the low hollow shadow of the couch.

Replacing the cork in the bottle, I sipped the last drops of liquid from the glass. As quietly as I could,

I put the bottle back into the refrigerator and pressed the white door shut.

On the street, despite the cold, I carried my coat draped over one arm, occasionally feeling the garment to make sure the pocketed instruments were secure. After many blocks I pulled the coat on, passing bars, variety stores, beauty salons, and a gas station.

Near the shelter of a bus stop, I paused to get my bearings. Inside the shelter with its see-through plastic wall stood a teenaged girl. She wore a small black hat with a veil over her eyes, a black coat, one black silk glove of the same consistency as the veil, a black leather skirt, stockings with heavy seams, and had an orange-tinted teased haircut.

She said, "Ya better not try nothin'."

We looked at each other for several seconds, then I turned my back to her, deciding to go down a small side street. As I stepped away her voice came over my shoulder.

"Ya just better not."

The little side street opened onto a round square where three other streets converged. In the center of the square was a war monument, a small column with an American eagle on top. The column listed the names of local men who died in World War Two. No other wars were mentioned.

On the far side of the square was a neighborhood market, its weekly specials announced in large block letters taped to the plate glass window. The sales this week were on ice cream, juices, and bread.

I pulled the instrument from my pocket and carefully traced the message between the door hinges and the burglar alarm.

TO HAVE THEM
ALLOW THEM
TO TOUCH YOU

Moving counterclockwise around the square I repeated the message on the side door of a gas station, the base of a barber pole, and the low windowsill of a beauty salon. Retracing my steps, I went quickly past the girl in the shelter, who moved her hands to her hips, but did not speak.

Back at the house, the smoke was diffused and stale, and I drew my sleeping bag close to the woman on the couch. As I began to sink, I felt her hand pass once through my hair and heard her voice say softly,

"It goes to show, ya never really know."

I'd grown used to the idiosyncrasies of the truck, to its desire to tilt right, its hesitancy in third gear, its instruments with their separate reality. Moving in light traffic over the expansion bridge connecting Boston to Chelsea, I had a brief sweeping view of the harbor and the islands that protected it stretching flat and pale to the horizon.

I was moving fast because I knew I would lose time in the labyrinth of Chelsea's streets; random byways with the pattern of pick-up sticks thrown by a spoiled child.

The poorest city in the state, the most densely populated, it was once a stronghold of immigrant Jews in the process of seizing the American dream. Now almost all the Jews and the dream were long gone to the suburbs, and Chelsea was a place of blowing litter, whores, truck yards, Puerto Ricans, Cambodians, and white trash. The elderly Jews who remained ventured out morosely, limping to local benches to nod and scan obituaries.

Atop this mixture, like sweet cheap frosting on a

71

stale cake, were the yuppies. Holed up in their condos behind home burglar alarms, they listened to their stereos, gentry in their castles, laughing at the peasants who frightened them so.

The gears banged down and I took the fish-hook curve of the Chelsea exit, went down a narrow street jammed with pedestrians, and stopped at a set of lights, knowing at once that I was lost.

Funneled toward the city hall by trucks and cars, I watched the swarthy faces watching me. The Spanish figures slouched as though under native sun, the cold not concerning them. I remembered something Puma once said. "Sunny countries are nice. People who live in sunny countries are not nice." I assumed it was true if Puma had said it, but I had never dwelled in sunny climes.

I drove around the diamond-shaped center of the downtown area of Chelsea once, then again, and on the second loop I was as confused as on the first. The street signs had either been removed for repair or were stolen. I tried a side street and came to a dead end.

I had three deliveries to make, two to offices sharing the same address; the third stop would be several small pieces for a barroom.

Backing into traffic, ignoring horns and gestures, I pulled to a curb asking directions. I was given pure smiles, empty gestures, foreign words.

I tried again, this time getting out of the truck to make an unsuccessful tour of a convenience store, drawing blank stares, shrugs, and wishes for a nice day.

Knowing that Chelsea was only 1.8 square miles, I was considering a random drive through the place as I walked back to the truck. Calling the office for directions would be futile; my ignorance of this city left me without points of reference. I couldn't tell them where I was, ergo they couldn't tell me which way to go.

Staring down the streets, trying to find something, anything that would connect the packages to their destination, I heard a voice come over my shoulder, clear and distinct, mocking a British accent.

"Doctor Livingstone, I presume?"

His German sports car was at a sharp angle to the curb, inches from the truck's front bumper. The driver's door of the car was open and he was leaning against the door of the truck, arms folded as he resumed speaking.

"It's fate, lad, fate, the only two white folks in the jungle stumble into one another. Not only that, but one is lost, the other awaiting his arrival. Stop me if you've read the book or seen the movie. Six rolls of adding machine tape, two ledger books essential for gouging tenants, and closest of all to my hymie heart, you have, I pray, brought the little gizmo that makes my cash register go ding ding ding?"

With that he pointed to the company logo on the side of the truck, then unfolded his arms and held between his outstretched hands a bumper sticker proclaiming the name of the bar I was seeking. The same bumper sticker was attached to the rear of the sports car.

He was tall, thin but fit, dark-complected with close cut black curly hair. His deep-brown eyes overflowed with energy and confidence. The impression he made suited the Biblical name he offered with his outstretched hand.

"David."

After I had grasped his hand he turned to gesture at the truck.

"I was at the bank and on your third orbit figured you might need directions. It would be easier to ride along than try to explain the streets. Mind?"

"Not at all."

Jamming the bumper sticker in his belt he pulled himself into the cab beside me. His car, being almost at a right angle to the curb in front of the truck, bothered me. I turned to him.

"You're going to leave it like that?"

His gaze went from the car to me and then to the litter tumbling in the frigid breeze.

"Why, do you think it will decrease property values?"

As we caught the flow of traffic, he pointed the way, accompanying his directions with quick doses of local history. One street we came to was blocked by wooden barricades. A lone fire engine stood guard in front of a burned tenement building; a red exclamation point to the block-wide ice sculpture.

David's hands framed the structure as we drove past.

"Fortunately, not one of my edifices. Quite a sight yesterday morning. About 600 Cambodian lads or perhaps Vietnamese, I never could tell the difference, running down the street holding their wide-screen color television sets. Terrible moments of panic as they squatted on the curb wondering why there was no picture on the screen. Several of the lads so upset they ran back into said burning edifice to see if perhaps mom or kids, understandably left behind in priority evacuation, had light to shed on the issue of blank screens. Tragedy further compounded by 800,000 homeless roaches, not to mention scores of rodents missing in action."

After a few more blocks we arrived at the building where two of the packages were to be delivered. David had his door open before the truck was at the curb, dismounting as I stopped the vehicle. The building was three stories high, and David told me the offices I wanted were on the third floor.

He got back in the cab as I pulled the bundles from the rear of the truck and went into the building. When I had made the deliveries I pushed the two-wheeler out of the building with one hand.

I stopped when I saw the truck was empty, checking once around the vehicle, even peering cautiously into the cab wondering if he were crouching down inside it.

"Up here, lad."

On the roof of the building, he was framed against

the sky, feet spread wide, arms raised above his head, seemingly unable to decide between flying up or down.

"What the hell are you doing?"

He spread his arms further apart, tilting his head back. He let his coat fall open to flap black against the pale sky, his arms rising almost vertical above him.

"Taking the lay of my kingdom, lad. What was it Satan said to that misguided Jewish fellow? 'If thou art the Son of God then cast thyself down and the angels will not allow thy foot to strike a stone. All you see before Thee will be Thine if Thou wouldst worship me!'"

He stepped onto the metal parapet of the roof, then, leaping back, shouted.

"Begone, Satan!"

He came back onto the parapet.

"How'd I do? Do I get to be in the Christmas play?"

"You're crazy."

"Yes, but I'm also rich, are you?"

"No."

"So who's crazy? I'll be right down."

In seconds he burst out of the building, coattails billowing behind as he clambered into the cab.

"Press on lad, only one stop left, and I happen to know where it is. It's a pub owned by a crazy rich Jew who doesn't drink."

We went through another square, this one bordered by bars, liquor stores, a Spanish market, and a police station. At the edge of the square he asked me to stop. I pulled the truck over to the side of the road as he pointed at a three-story building that seemed thin and frail, dwarfed by the nearby mammoth bridge carrying the interstate traffic.

"See that building?"

His finger was aimed at the house.

"Yes."

"This morning at 6:30 I went to see the fellow who lives there, lives being perhaps too generous a word, but anyway I went to see the fellow who has dwelled within said structure for six fucken months, never paying me a dime in rent, and at 6:31 ante meridian, I threw his fucken belongings off that porch, then I threw his worthless black ass out of that building. That, my boy, is how one is forced to do business in these troubled times. Know anyone looking for an apartment?"

"Not offhand."

I pulled back into the traffic as David raised one finger and began to recite part of a poem.

"Mere anarchy is loosed upon the world
The blood dimmed tide is loosed, and everywhere
The ceremony of innocence is drowned;
The best lack all conviction, while the worst
Are full of passionate intensity."

Trying to inch forward, a light turned against us and I stopped.

"The proof of the pudding, lad. But not to worry, we are almost to safe harbor."

The light went green and I followed his directions. We came to a dead-end cobblestoned street where the tongue of the sea lapped at the frozen roadway.

The bar stood on a corner opposite a bait and tackle shop. David waited behind me as I opened the back of the truck and tossed him three bundles. I followed as he entered the dimly-lit barroom, calling over his shoulder.

"Lunch is on me."

The place smelled of frying meat mixed with the stale promise of beer and perfume. He put the packages on the bar, then went behind the counter.

"I recommend the turf 'n' surf."

"Done."

He gestured to a waitress who came out of a dark corner of the room, dressed in black, her brunette hair in a long, twisting ponytail falling to her waist. Her face held onto its baby fat even as the lines of 30-plus years crept around her eyes and the corners of her mouth. She nodded as she took the order. Padding into the kitchen, she repeated the order to an unseen cook. David drummed fingers on the bar.

"Drink?"

"No thanks, I'm working."

"Ah, self-discipline. I like that." He paused. "Your first trip to our little kingdom of Chelsea?"

"First in a long time."

He leaned closer.

"Something for every taste here, lad. An up and coming community. A microcosm of the land of the free, the home of the brave. A place where a man can make his mark in the world. We have a government of open minds and similarly inclined palms; we have pimps, hookers, drug dealers. We even have our very own newspaper ever ready to cover any number of ribbon cuttings or Elks cake sales. Yessiree Bob, despite the best efforts of bad dope and good hand-guns, the population just grows and grows; why lad, a sensitive fellow could sit right here and watch America turn brown before his very own eyes."

Finished with words, he opened the packages one by one, pausing to carefully examine the piece that would fit into the cash register. Opening the side of the machine, he gently pressed the device to the guts of the machine and held it over an identical piece set inside.

Lifting the defective piece out, he set the new part in and shut the small green door on the side of the register. His lips moved silently, tiny beads of per-spiration forming on his forehead as he worked.

Exhaling, he relaxed, then pulled the roll of paper from its box and worked it into the register. Shutting the door he gave a few triumphant taps of the keys and the paper snaked out. He slammed the cash drawer, and the little bell rang.

"My favorite song," he announced as the food arrived.

As I ate he drew a glass of water from the tap, then sat on a stool behind the bar opposite me.

"As I said, I believe in fate. Our society is paralyzed by the obscenity of the so-called scientific process, but I am not part of that process; don't believe in it. Fate, lad, fate, omens and totems, such things rule mankind and always have. Ours is no different than the jungle societies we put in National Geographic to snicker at and ogle. But no snickering here, lad. You're welcome as spring rain or summer sun, whatever strikes your fancy. There's something for everyone in Fair Chelsea by the sea. And no, I am not a native, I evolved, some would say devolved, from a wealthy seaside suburb, but here I am, king of all I survey, the biggest fish in this here polluted pond, and right mighty thankful for the honor pardner, yippie-I-oh-kye-ay. It's just swell to sit here on my spread an' watch the ol' sun go down on what was once America. Yup, I reckon I'll spend my last days here pardner, ridin' a filly or two, an' a doin' what comes natural to a man, just a doin' what comes natural an' waitin' for the grandaddy of all pogroms to hit this here dad-blasted-infernal-God-fearin'-Jesus-lovin' promised land. And at the risk of sounding redundant I can only repeat, yippie-I-oh-kye-ay."

As he went on I listened, watching the sweat again begin to glisten on his face. When he finished I tapped the plate with the knife.

"Good food."

"The best, pardner. Your wife like to cook?"

"Did I say I was married?"

"No, but I'm sensitive. I can tell."

"Yeah, she's a wonderful cook."

"And you?"

"I bake."

I pointed the utensil at him.

"You married?"

"Oh, in a manner of speaking. In a modern way. In the way of the world, the way of all flesh. Yes, happily thank you; she's a wonderful girl. An American actually, from the Midwest. Been there?"

"Never." "Oh you should go. They have such wonderful street numbers. You know like ninety-two thousand six hundred and forty-five South Main Street. A certain strength, a certain Protestant moral certitude to such numbers. Perhaps that's why we're so sinful back here in the East. Maybe our numbers are just too low. Why, I just love to cruise those long white boulevards and pull into a gas station and say *Pardon mon ami, s'il vous plaît*, but where is number eight million two hundred fifty-seven thousand and fourteen? My in-laws live there.' And the fellow says, 'Hey you ain't no Jew-boy are ya? 'Cause if ya are, I'm gonna have to charge ya for the info. Haw, haw haw.'"

Beneath the sarcasm he seemed genuinely hurt as he continued.

"I do hope I don't sound resentful or unpatriotic, I mean I think our Mideast policy is just divine and I go to all the Rambo movies. I fly my M.I.A. flag, I get all my jokes from the *Reader's Digest*. I even read the *Playboy* interviews all the way through before I look at the pictures and jerk off, but well somehow, do you think that maybe . . ."

He dropped his voice to a whisper and leaned over the wooden bar.

"Do you think they suspect I'm not one of them?"

Before I could answer he snapped straight up.

"My favorite movie of all time is 'Cabaret.' A close second is 'The Sorrow and the Pity.' I think I died during the Holocaust. I think they killed me on Kristallnacht. I dream about the shattering glass, and I hear the voices singing in the dark. I can smell the beer on their breath, it's not an unpleasant smell. One of their hats fell on the floor of my shop. You know those hats with the little feathers in them, little feathers like the things fishermen use on their hooks?"

He was breathing heavily, his chest heaving, the perspiration drawing together in beads about his face. His eyes had been unfocused and now they came back to the room, and the odors of the place and the deep stained wooden bar, and his voice was like that of a child.

"You know the kinds of hats I mean don't you?"

"Yeah, I do."

"I'm glad you know. Would you like anything else? Ice cream, pastry, coffee?"

"No thanks. I have to get going, have to beat the rush over the bridge."

"Right, that makes sense."

"I'll stop in again. We'll talk."

At once he shook off the mood that had come upon him.

"Of course we will, pardner. Sit around the old campfire and jaw a spell. Mix a few potions perhaps, a drink for you, a treat for me. Can we shake on that?"

We clasped hands as he said, "Out here a man's word is law. Adios pardner."

I stopped on the way out and turned to him.

"What about your car?"

He smiled, "I have eight others."

Alone on the floor in silent darkness, the doubts and fears come. A man hears the creaks and groans of a building, the rapid tugs of the wind rattling the loose window in its sill.

At such times a man comes awake, his heart pumping. I remembered what a cop once told me. "They always kill the guy first." Puma taught me at such times to picture the Earth in the black void of space, to see the Sun and to see the spin of the blue and brown Earth. Puma said to recall that in the coldest winter it is summer in the other hemisphere, that our summer is their winter. He said too that at highest, brightest, noon, we should think of the fearful in the darkness and perhaps help them through their journey.

I felt hot in the sleeping bag and strained for a repeat of the noise that had brought me awake, but if it had ever been, it was now gone.

Across the room I could hear Frances' shallow breathing and, again the fingers of the wind at the loose window. The long minutes passed, but sleep would not come. In my mind's eye was an image of my wife, frightened and alone with our little boy. I could see her deep in the bed burrowed in the sheets and silent blankets, the woodstove exhaling into the dark blue Maine sky.

The feelings became saturated with want, want of the fragrance and cool touch of her body. I came out of the sleeping bag, padded across the cold floor and awkwardly twisted on my clothes. With my shirt draped over one shoulder, I went to the window, its closeness turning the glass rattle to a reassuring sound. Pulling on my clothes, I slipped two instruments into my pockets. Gathering a pair of warm socks, I put my boots on in the hall, so as not to awaken Frances.

On the street a bank clock told the darkness it was a little after 3:00 and I went down the street, twice stepping into shadow as police cars swept past. When I reckoned it was 3:30 I stopped.

Above, the elevated track of the subway was silent and would remain so for another two hours. Again checking the empty street, I strode toward the looming presence of the Catholic cathedral, feeling myself shrink as one does approaching a ship at dockside.

Lightly touching the wall once, I grasped the faded green drainpipe with one hand. The ornate walls were ideal for climbing, and at the fifteen-foot level I gained a ledge and from there the black hollow alcove of a stained glass window.

Waiting for my breathing to slow, I sat in the ebony hollow, watching the street, listening for any sign I had been seen. Nothing moved and overhead I could see Mars and Jupiter in vertical alignment with the waning Moon.

Lifting both legs, I pressed them hard against the opposite wall of the alcove and pulled the screwdriver and file from my pockets. The street remained unperturbed when the window popped open.

I pushed against the flow of warm musty air and gained the interior, gently pulling the colorful glass shut behind me. Breathing the inner warmth, not moving, I waited to see if I had caused alarm. But there was no sound, and as my eyes focused to the gloom, I saw that I was between the seventh and eighth stations of the cross.

In white marble clinging to the gray walls, the stations depicted Jesus falling for the second time, and His telling the women of Israel to weep not for Him, but for themselves and their children and their children's children.

Lowering myself, I found the top of the nearest pew to be more than a foot from my boots. The strain went up my arms and burned in my hands as I let go of the ledge and ended up on my back on the pew.

Getting up, I adjusted the strap that held the instruments and went to the nearby confessionals, pulling back the purple curtain that covered each wooden chamber. Convinced I was truly alone, I moved back up the center aisle, went into a pew, and squeezed around a yard-wide marble column.

Kneeling, I unrolled the instruments and grasped two that I knew could deal with the heavily lacquered top of the pew in front of me. One would penetrate the lacquer, the other deposit the message.

Still kneeling, I unrolled the cloth, laying the tools out on the pew in front of me. Before beginning, I looked at the altar, at the stained glass windows, at the gloom, in which, I knew, the ceiling arched and soared above. All was as it should be.

Breathing on my hands, I bent to the task, planning these letters so they could be felt as well as read.

As I worked, the heavy cold musk of the empty cathedral seemed to quiver, and I stopped and looked up. Crouching low I swept the shavings from the narrow pew top to the floor with one finger. There was no movement, no sound, but again I sensed a draft, sensed it not so much by moving breeze as through a deeper pungency to the air.

The message on the top of the pew came fairly easily and when I was satisfied, I scattered the shavings with my breath.

I took special care with the phrase that would be on the pews that fed into the confessionals. The work went quickly enough so that when I had left the phrase on two pews there was still no hint of the coming dawn. Rolling up the instruments to move to the far side of the cathedral I hesitated, and then heard a door boom shut somewhere behind the altar.

Ducking, I scrambled across half the length of the

church, then crawled behind a pillar. Keys rattled loudly and there came a set of footfalls sounding the solid gait of authority.

I stood up, my back pressed hard against the side of the pillar. The footsteps stopped, but there was no piercing beam of a flashlight, no crackling of a two-way radio. I squeezed the instruments in my fist, realizing I had dropped my gloves somewhere.

When it came, the voice was older, but with a subdued anger and sure resonance. He asked in Latin what I was doing.

"Quid faces?"

In the vast echoing building I did not have to raise my voice to answer.

"Narro veritam (Telling the truth)," I answered.

I heard him strike the match once, then twice before it flared, the yellow glow of the candle lifting the gloom, the flames of the second and third drawing forth the score of saints on the walls.

"I thought you were some damn crazy nigger."

"No."

"Id est evidens (That's obvious)."

He laughed, childlike.

"Pardon the racism, but we don't get too many little old ladies at 4 a.m."

The laughter came again, wet, light, completely divorced from the tired voice that now called out.

"Vene introba ad luminem (Come into the light)."

With the instruments in my right hand, and my left hand in my jacket pocket, I stepped from behind the pillar, and stood tight against the back of a pew. He was tall, angular, and wore his gray hair in a severe crew cut. We were nearly 100 feet apart and because of the candles, I could see him better than he could see me. Even so, his features were indistinct, seeming to waver in the flickering light.

He wore a black robe with the wide leather belt of his order. Beneath the robe I could see the thin line of a white t-shirt. He seemed a man used to the coarse whispers of insomnia.

He stood before the first of the three marble steps that led to the tabernacle. Arms folded, perhaps against the chill, he peered at me. I could discern black reading glasses and a gold chain around his neck. Connected with the face, the voice now seemed louder.

"Who taught you Latin?"

"Myself."

A sound passed from him, like a soft grunt of recognition.

"Catholic?"

"At one time."

He answered softly. "Weren't we all?"

Turning his back to me, he ascended the stairs. With a deft move he opened the small door of the tabernacle and pulled out a chalice. I sat down, noting the first hint of gray sky beginning to flush the colors of the windows. This time his voice was louder.

"Know what the ancient Greeks said?"

"What?"

"'Those who live near the temple laugh at the gods.'"

In the silence trailing his words the aroma of melting wax reached me. When again he spoke his voice was very low.

"Are you laughing?"

"No."

Lifting the robe slightly, he sat on the topmost of the three marble steps.

"Why did you learn Latin?"

"I was disoriented. I was looking for some sort of lineage, for a pattern to the events that had put me where I was."

"And where were you?"

"Korea."

"And did you study Korean?"

"No."

Hitting the walls, his laughter cluttered back and forth between us.

"Perfect. Jesus, you're an American all right." Controlling his laughter, he asked: "You were in the military?"

"Right."

"But not during the war, you're too young."

Now it was my voice that rose.

"The war never stopped."

He nodded, then rose, turning he went up the stairs. When he turned again, he had the chalice, and I could see his fingers grasped it as Rome decreed. He proffered it with one hand.

"Drink?"

"No, thank you."

Outside, I heard a motor running high and fast, but the pitch of the engine fell as the vehicle sped past and vanished. The priest sipped the wine, sat on the top step and took a long draught.

"What impressed you most about Korea?"

"The animals in the DMZ. They've been un-molested for years. They're not afraid, and they're beautiful. The flowers there are beautiful too."

"That all?"

"Strangers trying to kill you is impressive."

Smiling, he lifted the chalice and drained it, then spoke, his face hidden by the gold cup.

"Yes. I happened to be in Jordan in '67."

With a cloth he carefully wiped the liquid from the cup.

"Did you know the Israelis are not very nice?"

"I've heard."

He kissed the chalice.

"Not very nice at all."

Both of his hands came around the gold chalice and his fingers were spread wide, giving the goblet the appearance of a caged bird. He shifted slightly before speaking, the movement causing the reflected light of the candles to flare, then quickly fade on the curved sides of the chalice.

He drew himself up straight as though he was about to speak, but then his shoulders sagged and I thought I heard a sigh brush the walls of the building. In an instant he stiffened again, his voice much louder.

"How did you get in here?"

Keeping my gaze on him, I reached out to touch the nearby pillar with the fingers of my left hand, gauging how long it would take me to reach the open window.

"I'm here."

His voice was almost guttural when he replied.

"So am I."

Turning, he knelt before the tabernacle, then rose to ascend the stairs. When he had replaced the chalice he faced me, arms folded.

"And what truth are you telling us?"

I spoke the words I had left in his cathedral.

"I am without."

Long seconds passed and I found myself wishing for more light, for more air.

At length he spoke, his words a coarse stage whisper.

"That's it?"

He laughed, at first gently, softly, but then louder, and the laughter grew uneven and harsh. I did not want to speak again to this man. I had a sudden perception of physical danger, realizing that he could shoot me right now and receive nothing but adulation from the media and the cops.

Bending sideways, he brought one hand up to his eyes as though shading them from a harsh glare. He spoke again.

"Where are you, where'd you go?"

I didn't answer.

"Here's a line for ya, old buddy. 'Thou hast no

right to add anything to what Thou hadst said of old. Why then art Thou come to hinder us?'"

His voice rose. "Can you name that tune, friend? How about this one? 'Tomorrow I shall burn Thee. Dixi.'"

I went down on all fours and began crawling across the darkened floor toward the open window.

His voice came again, now louder than ever.

"Wait, aren't you going to kiss these bloodless lips?" His laughter slipped its chain, the cruelty in it drawing strength from the echoing walls. "You're not going to make it friend, they're already coming for you."

He saw me as soon as I stood beneath the open window. "Dostoevski, friend, old Fëdor was right on the money. You should show more respect for your elders, young man."

The drainpipe chilled, then burned my bare hands as I slid to the frozen earth, scanning the nearby storefront windows for the flash of blue lights. Pulled from a warm doughnut shop for trouble at a church, the cops would be ready to murder.

I sprinted across the hard lawn of the church, leaping the low black metal fence that surrounded it. Running in a burst along three blocks, I ducked into a doorway as two cruisers rushed past, bouncing blue strobes off each other's polished metal.

Calculating the time it would take the police to gather their information and express their outrage, I gambled on running straight home under the elevated subway.

It worked, and the chill that squeezed my body made the warm welcoming house and the grasp of the sleeping bag a delight. Even though I slept less than two hours, I met the day refreshed.

The morning the Banzai Bunny destroyed the Second Squad dawned with the warm, rich, flowing fragrance of early summer in the DMZ. The awful night when they seized the ship had become distant memory. We had rearranged the events in our collective consciousness so that they suited our needs.

In our retelling of the tale, especially to the new wide-eyed replacements, we had held the line with élan and wit. The paper shufflers and the brass had screwed up, but we, the unsung heroes, the grimy grunts, had saved the day. If the damn-fool navy could not hold on to its own damn ship, that was their problem. The infantry had hung tough.

On this particular morning we were doing what we were always doing. We were looking for infiltrators. The North Koreans dug tunnels under the DMZ, some of them large enough for men to run through three abreast. The infiltrators came through these, or they crawled like ghosts through our barbed wire and claymore mines, or they landed on the shores behind us in rubber rafts.

As we patrolled, we were actually within the DMZ. This was illegal, and against all the rules, but we were out to show we meant business.

I walked point for the patrol through the low shrubs, tiny flowers and sudden swift flowing streams of the Cease Fire Zone. Two hundred meters to my left, and slightly behind me, the Second Squad, made up of four men, moved in uneven spurts over the rough terrain.

The best description of patrolling I ever heard was from Sgt. "Diamond" Jim Dalton who sagely observed, "It's like playing guns when you were a kid, except it's real." How real it could be was indelibly impressed on my mind exactly nine days before the attack of The Banzai Bunny.

On that day at 3:00 a.m., or oh-three-hundred in military parlance, I was roused from a sound sleep by Sgt. Dalton and told to report to the company command bunker. There, I was joined by seven other young men, all as sleepy and confused as myself. We were all from different squads so we knew something very unusual was going on.

In a few minutes our company commander came in with another soldier who wore no insignia, but who from his demeanor was obviously an officer. This soldier informed us that the eight of us had volunteered for a special mission. We stiffened with pride for we knew at once that Diamond Jim had picked us from the 147 men of the company.

"Gentlemen," said the soldier without insignia, "today we are going to send a message to our friends in Pyongyang and to their puppet-masters in Moscow."

He told us we were going across the DMZ into

North Korea itself, and that once there we would "meet a friend." He said that at the present time there was no need for us to know more than that. We gathered our weapons and filed into the darkness behind Diamond Jim and the soldier without insignia.

Weapons taped for silence, faces blackened, we moved out swiftly. At first we went in quick march, then to double time. We stopped for barely one minute and the anonymous soldier told us we were at the edge of "The Z," and that a "corridor" had been cut through the barbed wire and mines for our convenience. We were to go through this corridor on a dead run.

We did just that and forty-five minutes later crouched on a small plateau. There among the scrub brush we lay in a wide circle all facing outward, waiting for our "friend."

And then, like a wisp of ground fog, he rose from a clump of bushes. In his 20's, of medium height, lean but muscular, he had blue eyes and blonde hair cut almost to his scalp. He wore blue jeans, combat boots, and a UCLA sweatshirt. We stared at his garb, too surprised to speak, nodding dumbly at his greeting,

"Mornin' all."

He was carrying a camouflaged case with straps of leather sewn lovingly along its top.

"Buffalo Bill," whispered Denny Duffy, who had nine days to live.

We followed Buffalo Bill, who followed the soldier without insignia, and we went north. Both Buffalo Bill and this soldier were relaxed and cheerful as we moved north in a long thin row.

When the sun rose, yellow and remote, we were a quarter mile inside North Korea. Buffalo Bill was beside me, and he unzipped the case with slow affection.

He lifted a beautiful walnut stocked rifle with a telescopic sight almost as long as the weapon's barrel. Humming softly, he attached a metal tripod to the weapon and handed me a pair of binoculars.

"Show time," was what he said.

From our position, the enemy nation unrolled below looking exactly like the land of our ally. I moved the binoculars slowly from left to right. It was like watching a smoky, silent movie. Beside me, Buffalo Bill was humming a Beatles tune as he prepared himself. Then he relaxed, and I peered through the glass as he spoke.

"Our North Korean buddies shot up a fishin' boat the other day. Now back home we call that downright rude."

He took a series of deep breaths.

"See them fellas workin' on that there wall?"

In the glass I could clearly see a group of workmen off in the distance adding cement to some sort of retaining wall. They seemed about a mile away, I said I could see them.

"See that fella leanin' on his shovel?"

The worker was the closest one to us; in fact, he was staring in our direction. I said I could see him.

The rifle cracked and the echo boomed once, then twice, but the workers were beyond the sound as I watched and the seconds passed.

The man leaning on the shovel was there and then there was a soft explosion of pink that went out from his head and over the other workers. I could see the tiny black dots of their open mouths, the almost comical panicked gestures, but I could not hear the screams as they dropped their tools to run in every direction.

The second shot seemed louder than the first as the workers scrambled up the steep incline, instinctively running for home. The one in the lead suddenly embraced the hillside and the others ran around him, disappearing from view and leaving the two dead men alone with the wall and the hill and the probing sunlight. Far off, so faint it seemed unrelated to us, a siren began to wail, and we turned south on the run.

By the time the rest of the Company was having breakfast, we had showered, shaved, been issued clean fatigues, and told to forget where we'd been and what we'd seen.

I was on a pile of sandbags lacing my boots when I sensed something behind me. It was Buffalo Bill. Yards behind him, hands clasped behind his back, gazing northward, was the soldier without insignia.

Buffalo Bill smiled and said, "We done good today."

The North Koreans did not respond, and soon things fell back to their usual pace.

On the ninth day after that incident, we were on patrol. We had two M-60 machine guns, one M-79 grenade launcher, M-16's, claymore mines, fragmentation grenades, smoke grenades, radios, helmets, and flak jackets.

At 9:30 on a sunny warm morning, a rabbit, a huge soft fluffy white rabbit, the biggest rabbit any of us had ever seen, exploded from the underbrush, and with a flying leap bounded off the arms and face of Paulo Cruz, knocking him down and jarring loose the pin of an M-36 fragmentation grenade.

Falling and screaming, Paulo slammed his rifle, which should have been on safety, but was on full automatic, onto a rock. The impact caused a burst of full automatic fire that tore through Denny Duffy, killing him instantly.

Amid the screams and groans of a dozen men, Cruz grabbed the live grenade from between his prone legs and flipped it blindly over his head. It landed between J. J. "James" Taylor, who hated music, and Marvin "Mad Dog" Minihane, who never said an angry word to anyone in his short life.

The grenade killed them both with a horrid muffled boom, causing Bubba "Mugga" Epps to shoot Paulo dead, because as he put it, "No man get fucked by a rabbit gonna stay onna same planet as me."

As the armored personnel carriers fired bursts of fifty caliber bullets into the high grass seeking to kill the infiltrators we said had ambushed us, and the medevacs circled, and above them the jets screamed, and the mortars pounded the earth in frustration, Diamond Jim sauntered over to where I sat, watching a file of ants, and he asked me,

"What did you see?"

"Nothing."

"That, my man, is the correct answer."

That night by the only paved road in the village, on the side of a shack that served as our whorehouse, I carved:

DID YOU DO GOOD TODAY?

The red light atop the green metal bridge reached upward and sent its message into the fog, an achingly slow cadence of warning. The cars moved in silence across the bridge, and their procession made the time uncertain. This feeling of time-lessness caused my throat to become tight, and tears filled my eyes while I watched the light and the way the red kissed the white mist.

But soon, I knew, someone would come into this men's room, so I quickly pulled out my instruments and in a neat scrawl wrote,

PEER WITHIN

Replacing the instruments, I went to the window and leaned against the cold unyielding sill as I breathed the frigid waterfront air of Chelsea. Below I could see a wet ancient cobblestoned street that led past warehouses straight to the water. Funny Chelsea. Curled against Boston like a baby to its mother. A tiny little place, where people were packed in like refugees on a tramp steamer. Boston was fifteen minutes and a world away across the Mystic Bridge.

Straightening my sweater to smooth the little bulge the instruments made, I strode back out to the high-ceilinged bar with its slowly spinning wooden fans, its rows of gesticulating men, and its waitresses, one of whom wore bright orange sneakers. It was she who gestured to me and whispered in my ear, "David wants to see you downstairs."

During our first meeting there had been a sense of inadequate time. He seemed to have much to say to me, and perhaps I to him. There had been such urgency, such energy crackling from him. His image had stayed with me, touching something within. Tall, muscular, intense, needing always to crowd one's personal space so that he filled his listener's view, David was imposing, almost charismatic, and I sensed too, almost insane. As I went down the stairs, I heard a steady crunching sound, a thumping of wood, and quick breathing.

The bar cellar was like the open basement of a house except that the ceilings were higher. David sat on a stool beneath a single bare light bulb. Two piles of money were before him on a small worn table. On his right, a pile of bills was heaped in a random mound; on his left was a stack of bills neatly arrayed. Near the counted bills were three straight lines of cocaine.

He gestured at a stool near the little table. Rolling

Checkout Receipt

Library name: M

Current time: 07/12/2016,13:16
Title: The vandal
Call number: MOLLOY
Item ID: 33206000723845
Date due: 7/26/2016,23:59

Current time: 07/12/2016,13:17
Title: On the come up [paperback]
Call number: HUNTER
Item ID: 33206007692936
Date due: 7/26/2016,23:59

Total checkouts for session:2
Total checkouts:2

Renew by phone at:
577-3977
or online at:
www.sanleandrolibrary.org

a ten dollar bill tightly, he passed it to me and said, "Partake, that we may speak."

I breathed in the line of white powder. I had never done it before. I felt a crispness of thought, a perceptible drop in body temperature. David raised his hand.

"Shhh."

I froze. He stared at the ceiling, as the floorboards creaked unceasingly with each movement of the customers.

"Know what that is?"

I waited as his gaze and his hands descended.

"To quote that great American and that simply marvelous anti-Semite, H. L. Mencken, 'The greatest collection of goose-steppers and poltroons ever assembled under one flag in Christendom. Boobus Americanus.'"

Grasping the edges of the table, he leaned closer, his hands clenching the wood, this throaty whisper adding urgency to his words.

"They'd kill us if they could get away with it. They'd love to cut our balls off, the cocksuckers."

He leaned back and began counting money again.

"Look at all this shit. A gift from the great unwashed."

He put the bills down, then rapidly wiped his hands on his pants.

"Christ."

Striding to a sink, he held up his hands.

"Look at this shit, just look at it. That's what

Freud said it represented, you know. Shit. Money's shit. It's filthy. I gotta wash my hands every five fucken minutes, or I'd smell like a sewer. Did you ever know you got so dirty counting money?"

I shrugged. "I never had enough to get dirty counting it."

He came back under the light bulb rubbing his hands. "Of course you didn't. Because you're a good Christian. You were too busy jerkin' off to make any. Here."

He flipped a fifty to me. I pushed it into my shirt pocket.

"Thanks."

"Don't mention it."

Like a child with leaves, he ran his hands through the loose bills.

"Shit, says Freud. That cocksucking coke-head. Blew enough snow to kill a horse. Did you know he was fucking his sister-in-law for 20 years?"

"No."

He leaned still closer.

"Of course you didn't. The little hymie prick. His whole philosophy was a coke-rap."

Now David's voice rose so that he was almost shouting.

"A fucking coke-rap, and all the Christian assholes swallowed it, the fucken way cunts swallow cum. Except the Catholic Church, except the Holy Fucken Roman Catholic Church. They jumped around like a bunch of old ladies who see a mouse. Holding up their skirts, screaming in terror. 'Sex!

Sex! Sex! Oh kill it! Somebody kill it, please kill it!'
The faggots, the Jesuit fucking fagots, sucking little
altar boys' pricks, 'cause they're not man enough to
rip a cunt's clothes off!" He squinted in the light, the
sweat more visible on him now, his voice again falling low.

"You hungry?"

"No."

"Sure? I'll have one of the girls bring something."

"No thanks."

Again his hands passed through the money. He
rolled another ten into a straw and passed it to me. I
inhaled long and deep, a sense of wellbeing, of
safety, coming over me as David spoke.

"I don't fuck with my girls. Lotsa pussy around, a
man don't hafta fuck the help."

He worked the money flat, the way an old baker
kneads dough. His voice rose again, and because he
was so close I leaned back on the stool.

"Know what half the pussy want? They want to
suck other pussy. That's what all these made-in-the-
shade-ultra-cool-yuppie-cunts want. They all want
to lick pussy."

Suddenly, he was almost screaming.

"And don't you forget that my friend, or you are
lost.
L-O-S-T, lost. And to quote another all-American
Jew-baiting member of the literati, motherfucker, 'O
lost and by the wind grieved, ghost come back.'
Thomas Wolfe, my friend, out of Asheville, North
Carolina, by way of Harvard, a path guaranteed to

produce a rare and fine blend of Christian gentleman, and say hey, speaking of Harvard,"

Again his voice rose almost to a scream.

"Ain't ya gonna tell me the Harvard Jews, Kissinger, Ellsberg, and Rostow, started the fucken Viet Nam War, ain't ya gonna pin that on us too?"

He jumped to his feet, scattering the money.

"Ain't ya gonna tell me the Jews started the war, but we wouldn't fight it, 'cause we're too busy defending Israel?"

He looked up at the ceiling, his eyes widening, and screamed.

"Don't you think I know what you're all saying?"

The sweat near his right eye caught the light as the liquid coalesced and a single drop fled down his cheek. He saw the feet descending the stairs before I did and frowned at the orange sneakers. Stopping halfway, the waitress bent over, both hands on her knees.

"Everything OK?"

With a wave he sought to dismiss her.

"Things here are going swimmingly. Tend to your flock, woman, tend to your flock."

She hesitated, took half a step away, then stopped.

"I heard shouting, I didn't know if . . ."

He cut her short, his neck muscles bulging as he yelled.

"You heard shouting, you stupid bitch, because I was shouting. Shouting is shouting. Remember the song, 'Shout shout, knock yourself out'? or am I dating myself? 'Shout' yelleth the Lord, 'and all things shall come unto thee. Amen."

She fled, taking the stairs two at a time. As David bent to pick up a dollar bill that had fallen on the floor, he noticed some cocaine ground into the heel of his hand. He held his hand at eye level beneath the light bulb. "How plebeian of me. How dreadfully common."

Licking the cocaine off, he sat down on the stool. Pulling a small paper packet from his shirt, he poured a gram of cocaine in a straight line, tapping the last few bits of the powder in silence. His lips pressed tight around a light blue razor blade, then released it to his hand, and he leaned close to chip rapidly at the hard white drug.

I could hear his breathing, could hear the groan that worked its way from deep in his chest and passed his throat. The sweat gathered, caressing both his cheeks. Chipping slower now, he said, "Jesus sweated blood at Gethsemane."

"Yes, so I'm told."

His gaze was locked on the white powder when he spoke. "My grandfather was a great man. A very great man. He fucked three different women every week, till he was over 80. He used to organize orgies between young boys and ladies of the evening and watch through a one-way mirror and beat off."

With the blade David continued to chop the powder, forming it into a circle, then a large single line, then four smaller ones. He swept and chopped, swept and chopped.

"My grandfather, my father's father, from whose loins I sprang, owned half of this city."

He raised his head, the tiny blade pinched between his thumb and forefinger, somehow menacing as his voice began to rise.

"Ya know how he got half this town? He got half of this fucken town by starting with a vacant lot and selling that for a shipment of wool waste, and then sold that for scrap metal. He bought a house, then another house, then another house, and anybody didn't pay their rent, my grandfather, that great man, threw them right the fuck out onto the fucken street, the colder the better, that's what a great man my grandfather was."

Trapped between his fingers and the hard wood of the table, the blue razor blade bent so that the reflections of the light bulb, and our faces, were stretched thin along the length of the blue polished steel.

"And at 83, just one day short of 84, that sainted man wandered down an alley in dear Chelsea and fell between a dumpster and one of his own buildings, and proceeded to rot right alongside the garbage of his Spanish tenants, although as he himself liked to say, 'What part of Spain they are from we do not know.' He lay there for two days and two nights until two little boys, two little uncircumcised Roman Catholic pricks named Morrisey and Angelino, found the body."

Deftly he plowed the powder into a triangle, then a long pleasant curving line.

"And do you know what those little Catholic cherubs said to officer Peter Nolan, Chelsea P.D. as that great man was being loaded into the wagon?"

"What did they say?"

He laid the razor down and whispered.

" 'Mister policeman, do we get a reward?' "

Above, the ceiling creaked beneath the shifting weight of the crowd. David sat, his head bowed, the sweat on his flesh seeming to evaporate as I watched, his hand absently tracing a cross in the white powder. "You understand these things. But of course you are descended from a noble race. The Celts. Loyal, fierce, despairing, and absolutely unforgiving; the latter a trait, I fear, God Himself is rather long on."

Lifting his gaze, he blinked at the room, and continued in a gentle voice.

"Come along, lad, let us see the sights that must be seen."

I went first up the stairs, ascending into the smoke and noise and the inquisitive looks of some of the patrons. We left the bar through the back door. David's mood suddenly lifted as he skipped down the wooden stairs and onto the cobblestoned street.

The cold seized me, so that my breath came shallow and rapid, but David strode forward. We entered a darkened warehouse that was mercifully warmer, and in the dizzying blue-black darkness I followed his booming voice.

"Step lively, lad, step lively."

We went upstairs. I stumbled several times, leaning heavily against the wall, for there was no railing. We went on in darkness to a second level of the warehouse. He stopped, and as my eyes adjusted to the gloom, I could see his right arm raised, calling for me to be still.

Softly he said, "One of my buildings. I have 51, thanks to my sainted grandfather. I buy and sell them as you once played Monopoly. The difference being, I always win the game."

We went across the dry expanse of the room, to a narrow corridor that turned into an enclosed catwalk connecting to the next building. We crossed, David pushing hard against a metal bar that opened the kelly green door of the new building.

Now we were in an empty wood-scented room, as dim as, but even larger than, the one we had just left. I could see large canvasses on the wall, and abstract sculptures were stationed in the open space like the tiny, desperate trees that clutch the inlets of Maine.

The only light came from two night-lights plugged into the wall at ankle height. As I followed David past them, I saw that the plastic cover of each had been molded into the face of a woman, her finger raised to her lips, calling for silence.

Suddenly David disappeared into a side hallway, and as I caught up to him, I could see at the end of the hall a thin bar of light clearly defining the borders of a closed door. As we drew closer, the heavy fragrance of scented candles and incense clung to the wooden walls.

Drawing staccato bursts of air into both nostrils, David advanced upon the door. Halting before it, he again sniffed at the darkness; then rapped twice on the door with his knuckles.

"Are we decent? Are we being good girls?"

A woman's voice answered, deep and sure.

"Fuck you, David. Fuck you and the horse you came in on!"

Deftly, with one hand, like a detective in the movies, David snapped a credit card from his back pocket, and sliding it into the door jamb, snapped open the interior lock. He opened it with a gentle nudge of his foot.

From the bed, two naked women stared at him, the brunette on the right furious, the smaller auburn-haired woman on the left, seemingly thrilled. As he spoke, I stepped into the room to the left and slightly behind him.

"Horse? Dear woman, the stork brought me. Or did you think our being here was accomplished by something as vulgar as a man fucking a woman?"

Two plumes of smoke whooshed from the brunette's nostrils, expanding and rolling the length of the sheet.

"Fuck you, David."

He puts both hands to his ears.

"Oh, there's that awful F word again! You know how it upsets me!"

He made a slight turn in my direction. "Now ladies, may I introduce . . ."

Snapping back the covers, the brunette cut him short as she came out of the bed, her back to us, and stood. She walked slowly, deliberately, to where her bathrobe was draped over a radiator. As she moved with controlled fury, I noticed her body, at least the back of it, was without a single imperfection.

With the robe on she turned to face us, the cigarette clinging to her lower lip. She seemed about to speak, but then shrank back against the metal radiator, glaring at David. In the bed, the face of the other woman was brimming with delight. Shorter, fuller, sexier than the brunette, she was riding her sexuality with the careless aplomb of a skilled surfer on a growing wave. She caught David's gaze and held it, making the other angrier, and David spoke only to the woman in the bed.

"As I was saying, this man is an artist, of exactly what art form I am unsure, but as someone, no doubt a hebe, once said, 'I know one when I see one.'"

I introduced myself to the woman in the bed who beckoned me close and clasped my hand with a cool, firm grip. David introduced the brunette to me, and she didn't so much as nod. I told her I thought the room was lovely, which added a tinge of moroseness to her rage. I looked again about the room and thought that it really was quite pleasant.

Drifting in and out of focus with the waxy ebb and flow of the candles, the paintings were truly beautiful. They lined the walls, wide and sure, barely a foot from the floor, all of them depicting the same woman in nude repose, the same auburn-haired woman I had just introduced myself to.

Like mirrors, the paintings reflected her, each canvas a frozen moment of her, as she rolled over in the bed, the last canvas beside the first, nearly identical but for the locks of hair let loose by the movements of the painted figure.

David struck the match that lit the marijuana cigarette on his lips. He took a luxuriant drag of smoke, and with the cigarette behind his back, walked the wide wooden floor planks like an old sea captain as he spoke.

"An artist was giving an exhibition of his paintings in Boston, and a lady from Beacon Hill said to him, 'I like your work, but what are you trying to say?' And he said, 'Lady, if I could say it do you think I'd bother painting it?'"

At that, even the brunette smiled, the expression testing and fleeing her face like a nervous sparrow from a branch. But then she looked closely at David and her features froze.

"Don't you ever take off that beanie?"

He touched the yarmulke lightly with one hand.

"I wear it in God's presence. And what gives greater glory to God than the body of a beautiful woman?"

The auburn-haired girl stood up, holding the sheets over herself so that only a small bit of her shoulders was exposed.

"Oh, do you really think so?"

He proffered the marijuana to her.

"Most assuredly, my little Episcopalian flower. Most assuredly."

She turned to me. "Do you agree?"

I glanced at the others, then at the long, low row of paintings. Looking back at her I could not form any words, and I nodded without speaking.

With one hand she pulled on the sheet so that it slid lower around her shoulders. Grasping it tight like an evening gown, she looked at the brunette and then let the sheet fall in a pile of shrinking white silence around her feet. We all stared.

"Then it's unanimous," she said, "and that makes me happy." She looked at all of us.

" 'Cause I'm a Libra, and Libras like harmony and having everyone get along."

Both women regarded him with curiosity as David moved toward the woman on the bed, the marijuana smoke twisting in his wake, like the incense of ancient ceremony. She seemed to stop breathing as he stood before her.

Slowly his hand reached out for her and their eyes locked, then he lifted her hand and gently kissed it, letting it fall back against her thigh. Then he turned to me.

"Come, lad."

That was all he said and I followed him from the room. Walking faster, we passed through the dim expanse of the building, down a flight of old, dry, complaining stairs, and down to the street. He walked rapidly right to the water's edge before speaking.

"I was afraid of her."

He turned to test my expression before continuing.

"They have such power."

"I know."

He nodded once, his eyes on the water, its ebony surface still, its anticipatory grip making me step back just as he spoke again.

"Truly they do. Truly they do."

Like some sort of child's toy, the air horn of a truck sounded on the distant bridge, but the fog hid the vehicle.

David went on, "It takes a man . . ." He corrected himself and continued. "It should take a man years to appreciate their power, their world, their great, oh my dear friend, the great depth of their sexuality. Far greater than our own, far, far greater, and ever so complex. I do truly, truly I say, believe they wander in that sexual world, that deep sexual world, and we can only sit and imagine."

I heard the screech of rubber on asphalt as somewhere beyond the buildings an automobile roared in acceleration, and I heard the banging gears fade in the ever growing distance. David was looking at me as he spoke.

"So tell me," he gestured with one hand turning full to face me, "do you think I'm queer?"

"No."

"Thank you."

At his feet the water lapped the stones in a nervous, uncertain manner, and we both stared at the sound. No other noise came from the harbor, no machine moved. It was as though we were inside a vast, foggy hall while the drizzle began to cling and make itself felt, but then it may have been clinging to us all along.

The drizzle was on everything, it was a thin sheen even on the fog itself when he spoke.

"Why did you come here?" I simply said, "I'm here."

Silent, frantic, permeating, the drizzle moved within the fog and he stared at me for long seconds, before glancing again at the water that flowed between us and Boston.

As we walked back toward the bar I hummed a sea chanty about a young boy on his first fishing trip along the shoals of the Irish Coast.

Again we went through the bar, and David checked the register and locked the door of the basement. He picked up a motorcycle helmet and we went outside again. David carried the black helmet as though it were a great weight, and as he slid onto his motorcycle he held the glistening helmet up with both hands and said no Jew should be without one.

With a phlegmatic mutter, the machine came to life and its amber lights were beautiful in the fog. He didn't wave and the street held the machine's sounds long after he had vanished.

I walked on, making sure my instruments were properly protected and dry before stopping in the pale light of an all night coffee shop. Inside was a

man with Tourette's Syndrome, gyrating within his
baggy clothes, his coffee placid and cooling before
him. On the wooden façade that would track the
path of tomorrow's sun, I carefully traced the message I had left in Maine.

BEWARE LOVE

The previous night we had carried the tree lengthwise between us, she clutching the tip, my bare hands around the base with its sticky sap and fresh wound. Its fragrance was from childhood when the nights were longer, colder, and ever so much darker.

The crowds, the uneven sidewalks, and the pockets of hardened snow made our movements awkward, and we stumbled like soldiers with a wounded comrade; but she was laughing with each step. She said that because we had waited until the last minute and got the tree so cheap the guy probably thought we were Jews.

Near the apartment the crowds thinned, and she held the tree with one hand behind her back and she spoke looking straight ahead.

"My Old Man used to get nice at Christmas. He'd drink like always, but he didn't hit nobody an' he used to sing all them old time Christmas songs. The Old Man, he had a great voice, he really did, even Ma used to say that, she'd say 'He's got the pipes, ol' John Thomas does, he's got the pipes.'"

She switched the tree to her other hand.

"God, did I ever believe in Santa Claus; jeez I guess I was a fanatic or somethin'."

With one hand in her pocket she continued.

"I got one brother still alive, that's all the family I got left. But me an' him was never close. I had another brother, Bobby, but he got killed in a car crash, him an' his dog together. He loved that old dog, can ya imagine? The brother I got left, he's way out to the west coast. I don't know how they can be happy at Christmas if it ain't even cold or snowin' or nothin'."

We raised the tree and adorned it with ornaments and a single strand of green and red lights she kept stored wrapped in white paper inside a long wooden box. Afterwards, we sat on the floor with the lights dimmed and drank a single glass of wine each.

Framed by the glass window, the new snow took on a bluish hue. We had agreed there would not be an exchange of gifts between us, but instead, we would try to be thoughtful, one of the other, for as long as we knew each other. She had insisted that we shake hands and cross our hearts to seal the agreement.

Christmas Day arrived within a metallic gray sky that deepened to pale blue as it embraced the frozen ground and the ice-covered river that ran through the city.

When my eyes opened she was sitting on the floor beside me, a red Christmas hat with a white tassel on her head.

"What am I?"

"An elf."

"Who do I work for?"

"Santa." She smiled and pulled a candy cane from the pocket of her housecoat and stuck it in my mouth.

"Give the man a Kewpie doll."

I fell back into the sleeping bag.

"Time?"

"Five-thirty."

"Jesus Christ."

"Watch your language, it's Christmas."

I lay for about a minute sliding back into sleep when she pulled my left eyelid open with the edge of her thumb.

"Gonna call your wife today?"

"No."

"Just checkin'."

As sleep came I could hear her singing Christmas carols in a beautiful voice. She sang Silent Night in flawless German and Adeste Fidelis in Latin, using the pronunciation of the Roman Church.

When I awoke, the sunlight was a cold yellow smudge on the glass of the window as the heat in the pipes and hollows of the house rose from below, passed upward and vanished.

The woman had left and I went out onto the back porch where the snow had worked into the porch screen so that the thin metal seemed as if it would break if a single finger touched it.

The day had too many memories that were an

effort to keep at bay, and I decided on a run around the frozen Charles River. The distance was five miles with not another soul present, and that seemed to please the ghosts, who stopped their whispers. I prayed as I ran for my parents, for my wife and little boy, and for the young men dead in battle with the second hands of their expensive watches sweeping on and on. I prayed my country would find its way.

Afterward I bought a bar of chocolate at a little store that was open despite the day. Breaking the candy into pieces I placed them on a metal tray in Frances' parlor.

I was lost in a book when she came through the door, cheeks flushed, a wide smile on her face. The cold wafted around her as she pulled a light blue hat off her head.

"I woke the turkey up!"

"What turkey?"

"My brother out on the Coast. It was even earlier out there than here; it's the time in the mountains or somethin'. Anyway, I woke him up an' told him I loved him, an' guess what?"

"What?"

"He said he loved me too and then we both cried!"

"That's nice."

"Yeah, 'cept it cost me about a million bucks in quarters, but what the hell, next time I'll call collect, but what the hell."

She stiffened as though someone had poked her.

"Hey, ya know I could go out there sometime."

"Sure could."

"Or he could come back here."

"Another solid option."

"I could even like fly out for a couple of days."

"Why not?" She broke into another wide grin.

"This is a nice Christmas."

While she hung up her coat I started to make coffee and told her about the chocolates. When she spoke again her words were muffled by the handful of candy in her mouth.

"He said he never thought I liked him! Can ya imagine? The turkey. I always thought he didn't like me. 'Course that's different, I'm a girl, anyway we got that straightened out."

One by one she touched the tips of five fingers to her lips.

"Jeez I ain't had chocolate in a dog's age."

Lifting another handful of candy she spoke, her words again struggling through the sweets.

"More people oughta talk, ya know? I mean what the hell, words don't cost nothin."

Sitting on her couch she lightly touched the corners of her mouth. "Ain't there nobody ya want to call? I mean it is Christmas."

"No. Nobody at all, not today anyway."

She shrugged. "I'm getting' together with some pals down at Mac's Pub. It ain't open today, but I know the owner. Ya know, have a little Christmas cheer, wanna come?"

"Thanks anyway, but I'll stay here."

"OK suit yourself."

She showered and changed her clothes, asking

several times if her hair looked all right and if she was getting fat. When she was satisfied she looked all right she left.

In the empty rooms I read a book about astronomy, and later studied a book of Latin grammar. The afternoon came and went quickly. As the sun grew fainter, I listened to the Christmas music on several different radio stations.

The music went on for long periods as though someone had left a tape on and gone home for the day. When the fullness of night came down I walked among the tall buildings and the lights of red and blue.

On one corner a man who had been selling Christmas trees stood with his hands in his pockets looking up the street whistling happily. I moved on to a street that looked over the river and took out an instrument. High above, a silent jet traced a pale contrail above thin clouds and below a quarter moon. The words on the wall were very small.

ONE AND ONE IS ONE

Edging the truck onto the moody asphalt of a school yard, I drove slowly over the grounds, aware of the rows of faces turning to gape in the windows above.

I had a number of parcels to deliver here, some large, some small, all smothered beneath layers of thick, brown wrapping tape, all bearing the name of the school principal.

Admitted to the building I took in its chaotic ambience, girls striding like whores on the prowl, boys overwhelmed and vulnerable to the marauding females. The air was stagnant with interwoven layers of five & dime perfume, waves of aftershave, and the kind of permeating, sticky-sweet stink that only silent panic produces.

I was at the end of the corridor near the principal's office when he popped out of the door and came striding toward me. Short, chubby, cherubic, he wore a neatly tailored gray wool suit, with a vest and a thick gold watch chain tucked into one pocket. As he walked toward me he looked back over one shoulder, then the other.

Reaching my side he pulled out the gold watch

saying, "That was quick. How's the traffic, how's tricks?"

I handed him a jumble of small packages, explaining that there were lots more back in the truck. But he didn't go back to the office; instead he tagged behind as I returned to the truck. When I jumped up into the back, he pressed close, leaning on the vehicle's metal platform, the little packages still in his arms.

"Lovely, lovely, nice interior. Once I pitied the manual laborer, now I envy him. Give me the tangible results, yessiree Bob. The immediate results please. Call me Pavlovian, call me irresponsible, call me unreliable, but don't call me late for dinner."

The bundles I was stacking weighed over 50 pounds each, but I found myself holding one of them and staring at him.

He spoke. "Crazy? Me? Oh not at all. But please do hurry. The little motherfuckers will be changing classes soon."

I lowered a dolly to him and he stood it up on the asphalt. Hopping down, I placed the bundles on the dolly. He led the way, holding the school doors open with an elegant bow. His voice came above the squeaking of the cart as we walked.

"Goodness, a few years ago I wouldn't say hell or damn, now it's motherfucker this, motherfucker that. A black word originally you know. They're quite adroit with language in their own way. But sincerely, I can't see it taught. Black English that is,

I just can't see it taught as a separate language. Some people want to do that you know, some linguists and some educators."

We reached his office. He went in first, I followed with the dolly and he continued to speak.

"I mean sincerely and truly I just can't see some Ph.D. teaching a bunch of graduate students; you know with her hair in a bun and granny glasses on saying, "All right, class, our lesson for today is 'Hey bro, what the fuck happenin'?'I mean I just can't see it, can you?"

I said I could not.

He pulled out a blue velvet hanky, dabbing quickly at his brow.

"We'll never integrate, you know. It's a joke. I mean integration. It's really lost its hard-on. Oh God, there I go again. Why do I use such language? Well, if the shoe fits, wear it. I wasn't always like this, you know. At one time I ran a school."

I told him there were three more boxes. He pulled out the watch.

"Gee, that's swell," was what he said.

When I'd brought out the last of the boxes I jumped down pulling the rear door shut. As we walked he spoke.

"Know what the boys call the girls?"

"What?"

"Beasties."

"Really?"

"Yes indeed. So much for the women's movement.

The horny little cocksuckers." He tapped the side of his head.

"What's happened to me? I mean really, what's happened to that old gang of mine?"

We stacked the boxes with the others. He signed the receipt, then gestured for me to join him in the hallway. Above the entrance to the office was an oil portrait of Horace Mann. The principal stared at it as he pulled out his watch, then snapped the device shut and put it back into his pocket. He spoke to the portrait.

"Ah, if you knew what the gnu knew."

The bell shattered the emptiness of the corridor and for several seconds drowned out the noise of the teenagers who poured from every classroom. When the metal stopped banging against itself, the rush of the students was nearly overwhelming. Brown, white, black, they streamed past, till the principal, like a skilled fisherman, cast out with his short arm and collared a boy in jeans and black leather.

"Good morning, Mister Pappas, how are you today?"

"Huh?"

"Tell us, Mister Pappas, where is Europe anyway?"

The boy looked back and forth at the two of us as though the answer were darting between us.

"Europe?"

"The very same."

"I dunno, out west, like in China someplace?"

"Thank you, Mister Pappas."

Pleased he'd given a good answer, the youth smiled broadly and rejoined the flow of the corridor.

The little arm shot out again, snagging a black girl with a pink dress and wide gold looped earrings.

"Doris, tell me something."

"Yeah?"

"Who won the Second World War?"

Her smile was warm and broad. "Hey Mister Harris, you know I don't go for that history stuff."

He rose to his toes.

"Praise the Lord and pass the ammunition."

"Huh?"

"Here's another one, ready?"

She seemed delighted and said, "Shoot."

"What's five times five?"

She became even happier.

"Aw Mr. Harris, you know I don't do that numbers shit!"

"But Doris, you want to be an astronaut."

Her smile grew. "That's a fact, Mr. Harris."

He bent at the knees, strumming an imaginary ukulele and sang.

"Shine on, shine on harvest moon, up in the sky."

She rapped him on the arm.

"You a funny old dude, Mister Harris, you one funny old dude!"

He bowed at the waist and said,

"The first pregnant black astronaut."

"You got it Mister Harris!"

He stepped closer to her.

"Doris?"

"Yeah?"

"If you knew what the gnu knew." She clasped her hands together.

"You the funniest old dude inna world Mister Harris!"

He waved good-bye, humming "Stardust." She vanished and he said to himself, "The first pregnant black astronaut with a ninth grade education who don't go for that numbers shit."

The little man turned slowly on his heels, raising both his arms wide, catching with them a lumbering young man, well over six feet tall, with pale pockmarked skin, his hair cut short showing the pink scalp beneath.

"Arthur, old chap."

"Yo."

"Arthur, old friend, how long have you been with us?"

The pale blue eyes became unfocused, the long throat contracted and exhaled as though all moisture were being drained from it.

"Seven, no wait, eight years."

Mister Harris hooked thumbs into vest pockets.

"Are we sure?"

"Eight?"

"Nine."

The dim eyes widened showing a large pool of white.

"That a record?"

"And then some."

"Wow."

"You can say that again."

"Wow."

"Arthur?"

"Yo?"

The pudgy man almost whispered.

"Arthur?"

The giant youth's voice fell too.

"Yeah, Mister Harris?"

"What have you learned here in nine years?"

The little man rose on his toes as the youth's face became furrowed, sad, his eyes fell, then lifted and he and the little man looked at each other like strangers through smoked glass. Lost in his concentration and the passing seconds, the youth seemed to forget the question, something he confirmed by saying,

"Huh?"

"Arthur?"

"Yo?"

"Where are we going?"

Now the hall was emptying, quieting.

"Like you an' me Mister Harris?"

"No Art, ol' buddy, like our society. The U. S. of A. The Big P. X., Art, ol' pal, like where's the next station, and who's at the throttle? Know what I mean jelly bean?"

"Huh?" said Arthur.

"Goals, lad, destinations, times of arrival, modes of transportation, fuel consumption, tire pressure, azimuth, coordinates, load limits, check lists, and flight plans, I mean is Triple-A going to map the route for us or what?"

Arthur lit up.

"Hey, they do that! My old man took a trip to Texas once an' they gave 'em a map an' drew a big green line like all the way to Eagle Pass. All he hadda do was follow the green line. They even had little clocks up on top so you know when to change all your clocks. Bad huh?"

"The baddest."

Arthur became somewhat formal.

"Hey, nice chattin' and' I hope I helped ya out but I gotta get to class."

Mister Harris took one thumb from his vest and began to sing.

"Oh, the yellow rose of Texas
Is shinin' bright for me."

Arthur took a quick step back.

"Well I'll see ya on down the road."

Both little arms shot out expansively as the principal shuffled left, then right.

"She sparkles like a diamond
For all the world to see."

Arthur tripped over his own feet as he half turned, ready to flee.

"Take it easy, Mister Harris."

The boy vanished down the hall pulling a green fire door shut behind him. The hall was nearly empty now except for a group of hispanic students hurrying toward their class, casting a wary glance at the little man in the expensive suit who serenaded them as they passed.

"Midnight, one more figure comes creepin'
Green door, what's that secret you're keepin'?
There's an old piano and they play it hot
Behind the green door . . ."

The students went around a corner and up a flight of stairs, their footsteps like a many-hoofed animal in a stall.

In the new silence of the corridor I heard him sigh, and reminded him he had to sign the shipping papers that were back in his office.

We passed beneath the gaze of Horace Mann, and the principal waited until I entered the room before closing the door behind me. He picked up his phone and said, "Hold my calls."

Then he opened a small door and gestured me into a low-ceilinged anteroom. As we sat on facing chairs, he reached into a desk drawer and pulled out a bottle of Irish Mist.

"A habit I've acquired rather late in life."

He poured two glasses and as I sipped he swallowed his in a single gulp and said, "Ah if I knew what the gnu knew."

I handed him the form to sign, and he passed the shot glass to me. When he returned the paper I took a sip of the liquid.

He shrugged saying, "So what's new, anything good on TV tonight?"

"I gave it up for radio."

He nodded in quick agreement. "A superior medium, engages the imagination."

He raised his glass in a toast; I did the same.

"To superior media." He emptied his glass and quickly refilled it.

"I must confess, though, those rock videos scare the hell out of me. Are they the new short story form? I mean, have we gone from O. Henry to that stuff in one fell swoop, and say, just what is a fell swoop anyway? Remind me to look that up; remind me to tell someone to send a memo somewhere."

Drumming his fingers on the table he hummed a tune then looked closely at me.

"I wasn't always like this; you mustn't get that impression at all. Once I was wrapped tight and fully certified, not to mention accredited and affiliated. But now, well it's these kids, I mean I'm having these out-of-body serious depression symptoms and asking questions like where am I, and who am I, and what's going on. Am I making sense? I often wonder lately if I'm making sense. It comes from all those blank faces out there. I mean, I could be making perfect sense and those kids wouldn't know it. I mean, those are the walking wounded in the war with reality, and frankly, I miss the war on poverty, how 'bout you?"

Finishing the drink, I told him I had to go and we walked together through the empty corridors and out to the truck. He hummed a Gershwin tune and shook my hand, saying softly "Ah, if you knew what the gnu knew."

Near the school there was a one-storey brick building housing a pizza shop and a video store. I parked behind the structure and, using two instruments, left a message on the uneven bricks:

LISTEN

Morris occasionally tended bar in the tavern that David owned. Usually he worked the morning shift, when the door could be left open, when there were more delivery men to deal with than customers, when he could look through the window at the street.

In the wooden building behind the structure where the women loved and painted, David had an office with floor-to-ceiling sliding doors and pictures of himself, his father, and his father's father.

The room was heated by a pair of white electric heaters, and it looked out over Chelsea Creek where the tugs elbowed tankers so large they seemed ready to crush the little local streets and all the people on them. Flung across the creek was a small drawbridge connecting Chelsea to East Boston, and each car crossing it emitted a brief angry buzz as though frightened by the sudden view of water below hollow metal.

The diamond in Morris' ear reflected the glow of the flame of the brass oil lamp and a red bandanna held his shoulder-length hair in place. He rolled some marijuana and lightly touched the sides of the joint to his tongue, sealing the paper to the cannabis.

"Man, it wasn't the same country when I got back from 'Nam, folks had got downright nasty. There was a maximum of yellin' and a minimum of listnin'."

He struck a match that flared rich and yellow in the dim room, drew on the drug, and passed it to me. I took some as a group of cars went over the bridge sounding like distant aircraft. David declined the cigarette, saying he didn't like to mix his potions.

"Myself, I'd had enough of nasty and I didn't need any more," Morris continued, "especially from a bunch of potbellied polyester suburbanite motherfuckers." This time he held the joint as he spoke, the smoke coming up over his face, then spreading to fill the room.

"I bought a car for 150 bucks and went north. Stopped in New Hampshire, way up in the White Mountains, middle of nowhere, little town called Whitefield. Got a cabin on the side of a hill, just read, walked around, saw deer, even saw a bear once, big ol' black bear."

The joint failed as he passed it, and I relit it as he resumed speaking.

"Anyway after two months I'm beginning to feel better. I'm not scanning the tree line for snipers; I'm not lookin' for trip wires as I walk up the library steps, et cetera, et cetera. Then I decide to hit the road, see the country I have been theoretically and empirically defending."

I settled back in the chair as David took out an automatic bank card and began chopping at a little pile of cocaine.

"So me and my 150-buck car go off. I worked a month as a waiter in Atlanta, three months construction in Forth Worth, drove a truck in Kansas, hit Frisco and didn't do nothin but drink and screw college girls, went to Seattle an' drove a cab, then to Chicago to tend bar, then Detroit where I worked for General Motors for exactly two hours and twelve minutes. Man, did that ever suck. A year later I made it back to Massachusetts, stayed in the Berkshires doing carpentry and going to concerts all summer at Tanglewood. God, I love Tanglewood. I lived with a lady who was sixty. I really loved her; she helped me a lot, ya know we'd talk about death a lot. She was a widow an' I lost a lot of buddies in 'Nam."

David breathed deep as he passed a tightly rolled dollar along a thin line of cocaine, repeating the procedure over two more lines. He stood and lumbered to the sliding glass doors, opening them wide. A cold punch of air coming into the room flickered the flame and dissipated the smoke. He slammed the doors shut, both hands rubbing his upper arms.

"An entire year deep in Christian territory; it's a wonder the bastards didn't boil you in oil. Praise Jesus, you're safely back in the land of the Jew slumlord and the Irish building inspector."

Going to a small table where an ancient type-writer rested, David uncorked a bottle of Scotch whiskey. Pulling three shot glasses from a row of a dozen he nodded at the typewriter and spoke,

"There's a book in there just waiting to come out, I've got it outlined, it'll be a great work, a great work."

After passing out the glasses he sat back in his chair. The thin white heaters and the whiskey's aroma helped the room's warmth grow as Morris resumed his talk.

"Funny thing about back then in the '60's." He sniffed the glass, swirled the liquid twice and continued. "You know everybody was screamin' about the war. Everywhere I went people were really up and down about 'Nam; I mean people were upset."

David proffered his glass.

"Yes, I seem to remember some disagreement back there now that you mention it."

Morris took a small sip of liquor.

"Well, you know as I travelled and people found out I'd been over there, they'd tell me how pissed off they were at the hippies. 'Dirty hippies' they'd always say."

He took a longer drink. " 'Dirty hippies' this, 'dirty hippies' that, but ya know, none of 'em really gave a fuck bout the 'Nam. What was really sendin' 'em round the bend was the hippies, and you spell that s-e-x. The hippies were into sex. I mean black boys fucken white girls in the park an' smokin' weed and saying fuck, and even worse the girls were sayin' fuck, and girls didn't never say fuck before then and that's a fact."

Morris drained the shot glass, then held it high above his head letting opaque drops fall into his open mouth.

"I mean John Q. Public is watching this shit every night on the tube, I mean every fucken night, friend, an' he's seeing niggers with white girls, and Jane Fonda tellin' broads to 'say yes to men who say no,' an' all these gorgeous hippie chicks screwing like rabbits an' he's lookin over at the old lady, all 200 pounds of her, an' he's realizin' he's on the dock an' the ol' love boat done sailed, an the only ones on it are the niggers fucken the white girls, the college students, and Jane Fonda and her great boobs saying yes to men who say no, an', brothers, old John Q. is one pissed off motherfucker. Old John Q. was seeing red, 'cause the rules of gettin' laid had changed and nobody wanted to hear his opinion about it, least of all Jane Fonda and all them white girls screwin' all them niggers. An' that did it, that defined war and peace, if you said fuck, you were for peace and if you were married to 200 lbs. of boredom you were wavin' the flag. No shit, all the yellin' and screamin' wasn't about Nam, it was all about s-e-x."

He took a long toke on the marijuana. "Tell ya somethin' else, brothers." He passed the joint to me, the smoke seemed hotter now. "A guy ran for president, saying he'd end an unpopular war, said if he got elected he'd bring the troops home 'cause he knew the people wanted the war over. An' he did just that. Man's name was Dwight D. Eisenhower. An when poor ol' George McGovern said the same thing everyone thought the poor motherfucker was a commie. Yup, ol' Ike ended the war, an' brought the troops home, an' nobody burned no flags, or no draft cards, nobody trashed no dean's office, nobody was out callin' cops pigs, no construction workers beatin' on no college kids, cause it was just a dumb ol' war, not nothin' important, like niggers bangin' white girls, and ladies saying fuck."

The silence and the heat rose until David went to the sliding doors and opened them a crack to let in cooler air. The sound of a single car scurrying across the bridge came clearly over the water and into the room.

David shifted his weight from one leg to the other like a boxer getting ready for the ring. He dabbed at his nose with the back of one wrist.

"I think you've got something there, lad."

"Believe I do, brother Dave."

David plugged in an old record player and we listened to Mozart's Symphony 40 and 41 as he produced a chess board, saying that some people thought chess a manifestation of the Oedipus Complex because its goal was to overpower the king. Morris beat both of us easily.

When the matches were ended, I walked to the Chelsea train station to catch the last train rolling from the north toward Boston. On the empty platform I left a message.

The great light of the train grew, sweeping along

the discarded refuse of trackside and illuminating the words on the metal pole.

Crossing the bridge over the water I could see the city and the muffled roofs of neighborhoods beyond the tall buildings. In the cold empty space of North Station I left the message again and added it to the side wall of the X-rated cinema across the street, and to the state office building opposite.

DADDY HAD A DADDY TOO

The January day had been typical of such days in New England. A brief, furtive scene played out under a remote sun that blinded the eyes while giving the landscape its sharpest focus of the year. Always January passes quickly, like that brief morning time when the sleeper wakes, hesitates in bed, then sleeps again, to wake frightened and late for the day.

An hour after the sun had pulled its trailing pink hues into the solid black line of the horizon, I followed Frances Lawless through a supermarket. The warm neon whiteness within and the solid cold blackness without made the task at hand a pleasant one. Frances hovered over the cantaloupes.

"You're feelings ain't hurt 'cause I asked ya to get lost, are they?"

"Nope."

She hefted two cantaloupes, holding them in her open palms.

"I mean it's just for a while like, ya know, like midnight or like that."

"No problem."

At the counter where the pale grapes were clustered on kelly green cloth, she hesitated again.

"I mean he ain't stayin' over. I ain't hoppin' in the sack with 'em or nothin', but how am I gonna explain the guy in the sleeping bag on the floor? I can't say you're my brother, cause no offense or nothin', but there ain't no family resemblance."

I told her I understood. That I'd go to a movie or visit some book stores. When I finished she began talking about Charlie.

"He's not real handsome, but he talks real nice. He uses words real nice, some of 'em I don't understand, but he don't talk down, ya know?"

I said I did.

"Right, an' he's got nice shoulders, an' he's strong, an' he's polite, an' he likes to talk a lot sometimes, but that's OK 'cause I like to listen anyway, ya know?"

I nodded my understanding as we cruised down an aisle of breakfast foods.

"He dresses real sharp an' he's clean. I like guys who keep clean. He smells good too, not too much after shave, ya know, like some guys. You'd think they fell in a bottle of perfume or somethin'.

"So listen, I really like the guy, ya know. He's just cute, an' ya probably don't understand, but I wanna meet a nice guy, I really do, 'cause no offense or nothin' to your gender, an' pardon my French, but I'm really sick a meetin' assholes."

We swept past the meat and its white-aproned attendants, past the milk and cream, and turned up another aisle where I stopped by a worn red machine that ground coffee.

I measured out a pound of brown beans and poured them into the open top of the machine. Flipping a switch, I watched the fine rich powder pour into the bag. Frances stepped closer, so that her hair almost touched my shoulder as she spoke.

"I never told ya but ya make real good coffee in the mornin'."

"Thanks."

"Really, it's good, mine tastes like burned mud or somethin'."

"That's because you make instant."

"Well, I'm in a hurry, ya know?"

"Yeah."

Before sealing the bag, I held it to my face, inhaling the aroma, Frances did the same.

"Nice," was all she said.

Putting the coffee with the other goods in the cart I asked Frances where she had met Charlie.

"Well, like I said, he's in sales, an' he comes in every so often. He sells adding machines, stuff like that; his dad started the business."

As we plied the aisles she told me he was separated and the divorce was on the way. He liked snowmobiles and had a dune buggy too.

She added, "He goes up to New Hampshire an' rides his snowmobile way out in the woods, over lakes and everything, an' in the summer he's got a dune buggy down to Cape Cod. He knows all about fancy wines an' stuff like that. He's just smart, an' a gentleman. A little fresh maybe but a lot of girls like that, but me I'm thinkin' long term if ya know what I mean."

With a sudden surprising intensity she grabbed my arm, squeezing it through the cloth of the coat.

"An' he ain't gonna be here in the mornin' ya know? Least not yet he ain't. Like I said I'm thinkin' long term. For once I'm thinkin' ahead."

In another aisle she got yellow paper napkins for the table, and two boxes of mint cookies with chocolate covering. In another aisle she picked up a candle and the shopping was finished.

At the apartment I helped her spread the white tablecloth and set up the dinnerware. I placed the water and the coffee in the pot telling her all she had to do was switch on the gas and remember to keep the flame low.

Under the hot steam of the shower I made plans for the night. I would buy a book, read some of it in a Harvard Square coffee shop and go about my trade. Soaped and shampooed, I laid out clean clothes and in fifteen minutes was ready to leave.

I pocketed several instruments and went into the kitchen, where I reminded Frances again to keep the flame under the coffee low.

She said she would and asked if her hair looked all right. Even though I told her it looked fine, she frowned as she absently touched it. She looked about the room as though checking it before leaving on a trip, then she looked at me and spoke.

"Well I'll see ya in the funny papers."

"Have fun tonight."

"My hair look OK?"

"Fine."

"I look nervous?"

"No, you look fine."

"Honest?"

"Honest."

I went into the street walking the block to the subway, hunched against the damp cold. Walking at this time of the evening was one of the small joys of being a man. There is a near-invisibility to a man walking alone at night. He does not draw the notice that a woman does. And whether he wishes it or not, a man alone on a dark street invokes fear in almost all whom he approaches. He is given a wide berth and has a wonderful freedom. He's part promise, part menace. His face invisible, he is alone with his thoughts.

As I walked I thought of a message for the night. The even dips and rises of curbstones, the cold air, the empty streets were ideal for thought. When I had decided on the words, I stopped at a neighborhood tavern, its windows warmed by red and blue neon.

Men's faces turned when I opened the door, but then they all resumed their talk as on the television above helmeted figures on ice skates battled for an invisible puck. The barman came to me raising his eyebrows in silent query. I ordered a shot of whiskey with ginger ale on the side.

The smoke of the cigarettes was pungent as I cut

through it, my hands on the pocketed instruments, to leave a message in the men's room. I took a chance openly writing on the faded yellow plaster above the sink, but I was undetected.

Back at the bar I took half the whiskey in one gulp, feeling its heated promise spread through me like widening ripples on a pond surface. On the television the Boston team scored, and muttered approval moved along the dark wooden bar.

A man who had been sitting almost directly under the television set got up and went into the men's room. In a minute I saw him return and tap the man beside him on the shoulder and mouth the message from the wall. Both of them gave slow, approving nods.

I took the ginger ale through a straw and in two sips finished the whiskey and left. The fine heat of the whiskey carried me along as overhead a train clattered and sparked its way from the city.

Standing in the elevated station I watched the train as it sank, becoming invisible into its metal bed of red and green lights. My own train came from the opposite direction and with a whoosh opened its doors on a welcome little world of warmth.

Most of the passengers were teenagers, off on a Saturday night date, shifting nervously in their seats, whispering and giggling at their fellow passengers. At each stop the train, like a wheeled bellows, threw out heat into the night, drawing cold air and chilled people back into its bosom.

At length the machine plunged into its familiar

tunnel, stopping at the Park Street stop with its sudden burst of shops, smells, and piped-in music. Almost everyone got off. Soon we were hurtling onto the frigid open bridge that crossed the Charles River into Cambridge. The next stops were busy Kendall Square and sad Central Square—a dirty place much loved by the insane. I exited at Harvard Square, and on the street I dodged the ever-present young people with their pamphlets demanding immediate stops and starts to consummate issues in faraway lands.

I moved into a well-lit bookstore, spending time in a rear corner admiring a fine collection of maps. I passed on to a cool, dim ice cream parlor where I had a delicious sundae in a silver dish, the ice cream the color of emerald.

In another bookstore I picked up a remaindered hardcover edition of a Latin grammar text and a magazine about the stock market, something I follow very closely. What I have always loved about the market was its catholicity, its quivering action and reaction to every single thing anywhere, its beautiful unerring flow to its own level.

At the fringe of the Square, I moved along the darkened streets leaving my message at the entrance of a restaurant, the foyer of an apartment house, the lip of a mailbox. I came back to the Square itself, then strolled through Harvard Yard. Crossing Massachusetts Avenue, I used the instruments on the sill of a window of a small men's clothing store.

I reconnoitered the inside of another bookstore

that was filled with the humorless faces of the Left. Passing back outside I went down a small side street, leaving my words on a light post and a wall at the mouth of an alley behind a restaurant. I was pleased with that, for there was a dumpster in the alley and I knew many men who rode trash trucks to be well read, men who as a rule, knew the score.

Moving back onto the main street of the Square, Massachusetts Avenue, I was caught off guard by a young woman who handed me a pamphlet promising to lead me to inner peace. Folding it twice, I put it in my back pocket.

The cool breezes of the early evening had dissipated and now the cold was heavier, more sure. I passed down an alley leaving my words on a metal grate, then descended the stairs of a coffee house called Paris.

The subterranean room was tiny and hot, the waitress wearing a black sweater, black slacks, and sandals. She brought a demitasse cup and I took the liquid in tiny sips, reading the Latin text of the tale of the Minotaur.

More than an hour passed, and on the third cup of cappucino Icarus fell to the sea, but his father did not and I ordered pastry.

At length, I left the cafe and with the book tucked into my jeans at the small of my back, and my instruments secure, walked to downtown Boston. It was about five miles, a long canyon of urban sprawl, black, then Puerto Rican neighborhoods, the airy rush of MIT, then the Longfellow Bridge with its subway track in the middle leading across the river back to Boston.

As I trooped along Mass. Ave. I tried to picture the British marching along this very road in the chill pre-dawn of April 19, 1775, on their way to Lexington to seize American powder. The English boys must have been very cold, for April in New England has the empty promise of a pretty whore.

When I crossed to Boston I decided to walk the remaining three miles to the house. I arrived at thirty minutes past midnight. In the hall I stood quietly in the dark listening as the exertion of the march filled me with a sure feeling of accomplishment. There was no sound and I noticed no light came from beneath the door. I let myself into the kitchen. The air was still, the little room held within it the aroma of a cooked meal. Without turning on a light I went to the parlor, but froze when I saw Frances silhouetted against the window, her head down, shoulders slumped. She was sitting on the radiator. When she spoke I knew she'd been crying.

"Don't turn on no lights, OK?"

"What happened?"

She didn't raise her head.

"Mr. Wonderful beat the crap outta me."

In the kitchen I banged ice cubes from two trays, wrapped the ice in a towel and returned.

"Here hold this to your face."

"I'd like to cut his balls off."

"It'll make the swelling go down."

"I'd like to cut all your balls off."

For about a minute she sat still, the cold cloth to her face, her breath slow, softer than the gentle hiss of the radiator. She shifted her weight as drops of water slowly fell from the crumpled towel.

"What happened?"

Lowering the cloth, she turned painfully to face me, a single drop of water running up her arm. Even in the dark I could see the area around her left eye was already discolored. Before speaking, she pressed the cloth again to her face so that her mouth was hidden as she spoke.

"He came over an' he brought a bottle of cognac, 75 years old, no less, an' he looked like a million bucks."

She shifted her weight with difficulty and I realized not only her face had been battered.

"So we have a nice meal, real nice, an' like I expected, he did most of the talking. An we had the cognac, geez that stuff could burn a hole in your tonsils. So anyway the meal was real nice an' the cognac was good, even though it burned my stomach a little."

In the wall above her head the heating pipes tapped a message of reassuring warmth.

"So then I clean up the table, an' he helped me, an' I'm thinkin' 'Jeez this is great,' ya know? I'm thinkin, 'Don't blow it, girl, this is a nice guy.'"

She adjusted the towel and resumed talking.

"So we came in here to the parlor an' I'm sittin in the chair here, an' he's on the couch. An' he's tellin' me all about cognac, an' how you're supposed to hold the glass in your palm an' swirl it, so the heat from your hand makes the flavor come out, it's a bouquet or somethin' about a flower or somethin' like that."

I asked her if she wanted a drink or anything to eat, but she shook her head no and resumed her story.

"So I'm thinkin', 'Jeez, this guy's real smart, what's he see in me?' Ya know? I mean that's what I'm thinkin', but I'm feelin' good, 'cause I figure, 'Hey this is a nice guy.' Am I borin' ya? I'll stop if I'm borin' ya."

I told her I wasn't bored.

"So he's talkin' 'bout this an' that, an' then he gets onto politics an' stuff, an' he's talkin' about the Middle East, an' oil, an' Arabs an' stuff. Then he says, 'Know what we outta do over in Beirut?' An' I says, 'No what?,' an' he says, 'Nuke 'em.'"

"An' I says 'Huh?'"

"An' he says, 'Put a glow over 'em. Hit 'em with the big one. Nuke the bastards.'"

The patter of the pipes grew louder and drifted higher in the walls.

"An' I says, 'Ya mean drop an atomic bomb on Beirut?' An' he says, 'Ya got it kiddo.'"

"An' I says, 'Well I didn't go to college or nothin', but I know there's a lotta different kindsa people in there. There's Arabs, an' Christian Militias, an' guys called Druids or somethin' like that, an' Moslems who crouch down when they pray, an' some are on our side, an' some hate us,' though I said I didn't know who was who doin' all the shootin,' 'an' the Israelis are there, and them Syria guys, an' those guys that wear them scarves, an' that guy, that Ayatollah guy, who personally I don't like myself, he's got a hand in there too.' I says, 'Hey ya can't just drop a big bomb on everybody.'

"I says, 'I seen a show on TV once one night 'cause I had the flu, an' they explained it. There's all kindsa people there. Ya just can't drop an atomic bomb on everybody's head.'"

As I leaned against the wall I could feel the warmth of the pipes within.

"What did he say to that?"

She dropped her hands with the wet cloth onto her lap and looked at the towel as she spoke.

"He called me a dumb cunt."

The heat sounded below the floor and she spoke very softly over the sound.

"Jeez, that hurt."

Now she pressed the towel to her face with both hands.

"I told him not to use that language with me, an' he says he didn't come over to talk, he came over to get laid. He says the cognac cost a hundred bucks an' I should be grateful."

She stopped talking to shift her weight.

"So I told him what he could do with his cognac."

She drew a deep breath.

"He tells me I'm cute when I'm mad, an' trys to slap a make on me. I told him to get lost. Guess that's when it dawned on him I ain't gonna hop in the sack, an he just plain slapped the hell outta me. He's a big guy too, that Charlie is.

"An' when he's done knockin' me around he says he's gonna go on down to the corner bar there, have a few an' forget his wasted evenin'. That's what he called it, 'my wasted evenin'.'"

The human eye can detect sudden movement in darkness, but does not see very slow movement. And I moved very slowly when I had to move at all in the doorway between the bar and Charlie's car. For a firmer grip I had wound black masking tape around one end of the 38-inch lead pipe I was holding.

The light from the opened bar door spilled onto the sidewalk as Charlie drew his gray wool coat around him. He called a few mock insults to his buddies back inside and started walking toward his automobile.

From the dimness of Montresor's cellar, Poe tells us that it is essential to revenge that the victim be fully aware of the avenger. But that was a luxury I could not afford. So I contented myself with whispering his name as he passed. He turned to blink stupidly.

I slammed the end of the pipe into his solar plexus, pulling him into the doorway as he fell. In quick succession I got him on both floating ribs, both elbows, and one knee.

As I knelt beside him I pulled the single piece of white paper from my pocket. I had repeated on it the message I had left earlier that night in so many places. The words were clear, for I had used my best penmanship in creating them.

The warm air was coming out of his mouth with a groan, as with a gloved hand I tucked the words between his left cheek and gum. It was a message I had first heard on Nantucket, later in Vermont, and again along the shores of Maine.

SPEAK BUT TO IMPROVE THE SILENCE.

The birds hesitated on the sidewalk, the cold breeze turning the tips of their feathers as David's arm hung over them. He pumped his arm, faking shots with the roasted peanuts and the winged creatures turned and cooed with each movement.

He threw down a handful of nuts and the birds shoved and pecked, ignoring the heels of passersby. David spoke as he explored the paper bag for more nuts.

"A proper course of action, lad. Bear in mind that your Corporate Founder once used a whip to chase the money lenders from the Temple. So I'd say you're within your common-law rights as well as the bounds of legal precedent. Not to mention the asshole had it coming."

I took a peanut and cracked the shell, peeling off the thin brown skin before devouring the fruit and spoke.

"I wonder if he'll make the connection?"

David looked up, the bag balanced on his palm.

"And take it out on the lady?"

"Yeah."

"I doubt it. Guys like him never make connections. That's why they're guys like him."

The birds danced their patterns on the sidewalk, nibbling and discarding the shells of the peanuts as David dropped more fruit among them.

"Ah," he said, "to be a pigeon in Chelsea."

The benches we sat on were at a bus stop and as the bus approached, a hooker, who had said her name was Franny, turned away from the flow of traffic and sat beside us. She had on a red miniskirt and blue sweater beneath a cherry red raincoat. She was short and redheaded, with the full figure of a French Catholic schoolgirl.

"It's too cold today," she said. "No guys are out lookin', it's just too cold. It must be zero; it must be below freezin'."

As the bus passed she got up and strode right to the center of the street looking down the line of cars. The fifth car slowed, stopped, and Franny was gone.

"It's always darkest before the dawn," said David. Abruptly he looked up at me. "Stop kicking yourself because you dealt brutally with a brute. You did the right thing. But it was a felonious act so be careful to whom you mention it. Myself, I am an incorrigible gossip and rumor-monger but I shall stifle my natural urges in this case and tell no one."

"Thanks."

"Don't mention it."

"Speaking of felons, you must visit an urban oasis

with me tonight. An ideal spot for cleansing the mind and soul."

"What is it?"

"It is the world as it used to be. The world as it should be, a masculine island. One of the few left, a fragile ecosystem as yet undisturbed by the onslaught of feminism, whatever that is."

"I'll ask again. What is it?"

"Steam."

Like wax gargoyles slouching in a hot sun, the old, naked men sat on the wooden benches, palms flat on the wood as though contemplating hand-stands. The heat was rising, rising, so that it hurt a little to breathe, and I opened my mouth and swallowed the air. It was 120 degrees, or 140, or maybe it was 160. The moist heat was part of all of us, and it was reassuring to know that these old men had come to this room as boys and their fathers before them.

Younger men came in padding like naked cats, nodding in respect to the older ones who sometimes did and sometimes did not acknowledge the passing youth. When we had entered the room David had nodded, and both elders had acknowledged him. They had been talking, but now with the young men present they fell silent until the youths left the room.

One of the elders had a thin gold chain attached to a gold crucifix around his neck. The gold glistened moistly around his loose flesh. It was he who spoke.

"An' that was it with them. That was the end of me an' them."

The other pursed his lips slowly, richly. He nodded in agreement, adding his silent understanding. The speaker continued.

"That was the end. A great betrayal Anthony, a great betrayal an' I'm not the only one."

The acquiescence of the other was slower, almost morose, as the speaker continued, now louder.

"An' that music. I loved that music. I cried inside when I heard that music. Them songs don't belong in English; them ain't English songs."

The other picked up the thread of the speaker's thoughts hurling them down like a gauntlet, as he shouted "An' the Mass don't neither!"

The speaker almost leaped up, the chain flapping once against his chest.

"'Course it don't! A great betrayal an' to hell wit' all them ones an' all them priests an' them women givin' communion. Whoever heard a such a thing? That ain't what God wants. God don't want no woman on no altar, an' he sure in hell don't want no Mass an' singin' in English!"

He slapped the wooden bench with a wet towel that lay by his side.

"They bring back Latin, I go!"

He massaged both knees with his hands and spoke evenly while the rage stayed in his whitened fingertips.

"A great betrayal Anthony, a terrible thing they done."

The sweat was bitter, profuse, it was in our eyes, our mouths. This was a splendid, a merciless heat.

Even my hair was hot and I made my way to the big bucket of water, cupping my hands and pouring the liquid over my head. The water ran down my skin growing warm even as it flowed.

A few feet away David was on the bench, slouched against the stone wall, mindless of its intense heat as time passed, unmeasured in this windowless cubicle. At length David sighed and said to no one, "Beautiful."

The minutes slowed and went on, and the moisture came out of us. All eyes were closed to the heat's embrace, mouths were open slightly. I thought of my father dying so young, and of his father at 90. The voice seemed very far off.

"Anthony, give us some heat."

It came almost at once. The body recoiled in alarm, but then the flow of moisture took on its own reasoning and I slumped on the bench close to David who lay back in a hot, moist reverie, his mind, I sensed, wandering in boyhood.

After many minutes, through the opaque door that led to the showers, voices rose and as I opened my eyes I could see the agitated movement of white flesh beyond the glass. But here in the heat it seemed very far away, and I closed my eyes again, contemplating the heat-wrought numbness of my lips, when the door swung open and two of the young men came in. The one who spoke was respectful and sincere.

"Santino, Anthony, you come in a broad's mouth, you know, a broad sucks you off, you kiss her after?"

Drawing a deep breath Santino shook his head.

"Ya do not. A man don't kiss no woman after that. A fag kisses a woman after that. It's disgusting. Ya don't kiss her."

Spinning on the toes of one foot the naked young man slapped his friend on the arm.

"Ya hear that? A fag kisses a broad after. See, you don't know nothin'."

The friend protested as they disappeared through the door.

"But I like to kiss her after."

"'Cause you're a fucken fag, that's why."

But the argument didn't stop and the tone of the glass changed from all of the bodies that gathered on the other side. The volume of the noise grew and the door opened, as some young men stood in the shower room and others spilled into the heat room. One man, crew cut, with a moustache, and the only one genuinely angry, yelled.

"Ya don't kiss her after, ya don't, ya don't do it, it ain't done."

He overwhelmed the arguments of the other side which were,

"I love her, she likes me to."

A man no one knew yelled to no one in particular, "You're the fucken fags, you assholes!"

But no one listened to him. As quickly as it started the argument was almost over, and it died when Anthony said, "You're killin' the heat."

When they all went out to the shower room the heat again descended, seeming even hotter than before, and the four of us settled back. The awareness of cold wind in the black air outside made the heat a sensual thing, and the sweat and the salty numbness of our lips seemed proper.

I raised my hands to the ceiling and it was like holding them close to a flame as blood pulsed in the fingertips and the great heat flowed and flowed. I was beginning to need the relief of the shower room, but I stayed, looking at David whose body seemed temporarily empty of his being. The time went on and the thought of black air was thrilling.

Santino spoke and Anthony answered.

"A man don't do that."

"'Course he don't."

As the minutes slid past, the heat induced in us a growing heaviness. At length David spoke.

"What would the temperature be in Maine, lad?"

"I'd say about 20 below zero."

He nodded, then spoke, "A wonderful cleanliness to a temperature like that."

"Yes."

"A certain clarity of thought."

"Yes."

He glanced at me.

"So, you like our little hideaway?"

"Nice."

"Then you must have the full treatment. What the plebeians call, 'The whole nine yards.'"

He ambled out the door, the room's air trying to follow him. He was back in a few moments with the moustachioed man who before had been so angry. Now he smiled and said, "How ya doin', chief?"

David gestured toward a wooden table in one

corner of the steam room, and I lay on it as another man brought in a large bucket made of cedarwood. From the bucket of soapy water he produced a large brush explaining that it was made of oak leaves.

As I lay face down, he began lathering my head with the brush, massaging and working his way to the soles of my feet. The white lather soothed my flesh, and the muscles below it. The pungent odor filled my nostrils and the hands of the masseur moved in widening circles. As the soap covered me, inches thick, he said, "Sit up." When I did he said, "Brace yourself buddy, this is gonna be cold."

With a slight grunt he hefted the wooden bucket over my head. The frigid shock of the cold water sucked the air from my lungs, scaring me so that I gasped aloud as the water continued to pour, chilly and plentiful. When it trickled to a stop I felt cleaner, fresher, healthier, than I ever remembered feeling, and he said, "How ya feel, pal?"

I said I felt wonderful and he told me that was the whole idea.

We left the room and David held the door open, saying, "Now we get sheets and sit down and relax. The sheets let the heat out real slow. You don't want to let the heat out too fast; you don't want it to stay inside either, so we get the sheets and we let the heat out nice and slow."

Picking up the sheets at a counter we entered a lounge lined with big green easy chairs, and in these chairs, wrapped like survivors from the sea, we lay among the other men just below a thin bluish layer of cigar smoke.

Close by, two elders spoke of frozen ponds and the color of ice in childhood. One remembered blue-black with sharp white slashes, while the other recalled very light green. Both knew the winters were much colder then.

David and I did not speak but rather became monitors of all other conversation. We breathed the traces of cigar smoke and heard all the words. We nearly fell asleep, and as the sheet around me became cold I knew the time had come to leave.

After great comfort or vigorous exercise, there is a silent glory to clothes as they are put on. Not mere covering, at such times they become a wonderful extension of the body itself, the colors and richness of the clothing interacting with the spirit, adding to its well-being. That was how I felt as we stepped into the solid mass of the New England night.

As we walked, smokestacks and chimneys offered their grays and whites in straight streams flowing to the skies. I told David it was time for me to leave and he asked, "Maine?" and I said "Yeah, Maine."

We shared an aversion to overlong good-byes, and with a few words and a quick handshake we parted.

I have long thought that the natural forces that bring people together provide the same ease of departure through mutual understanding. That was the thought I held as I prepared to say good-bye to Frances. She nodded as though expecting it all along.

Then she brought a pack of cigarettes up to her

mouth, a book of matches tucked into the cel-
lophane. With the fingers of one hand she pulled out
a butt, lit it and spoke as she examined the pack.

"So another guy's walkin' outta my life."

"Guess so."

She turned the pack on its side squinting as
though reading a secret message.

"Men. You're all assholes, an' I don't think I'm
givin' away nothin' top secret by tellin' ya that."

"Guess not."

She nodded, then looked up at me, the tears
gently forming at the corners of her eyes to fall
exquisitely down her cheeks. She took a step and we
embraced, her head against my chest, the sobs shaking her, until she whispered one word.

"Shit."

"They won't let you into Heaven if you don't stop
swearing."

She laughed softly and with one hand on my
shoulder pushed herself back.

"Hey, I been there once or twice."

"I can imagine."

"No ya can't but that's another story."

She put her arms around my neck, kissing me
once on the cheek.

"Pardon my French, but will ya just screw off
before I start bawlin' an' maybe don't stop for a
freaken week?"

I put my hand on the back of her head and kissed
her hair.

"Don't give up."

"I ain't gonna."

"You deserve someone nice, you'll find him."

"Promise?"

"Promise."

"Cross your heart?"

"Cross my heart."

Because neither of us wanted to cry in front of the other, we parted with a final glance and a small wave. In the darkness of the streets the cold sucked away her scent from my hands and as I walked it sucked away the taste and smell of the city itself, a sure sign that it was time to go.

With the instruments slung over my shoulder, I slipped the walkman around my neck, passing rapidly through the empty twisting winter streets, then under the steel girders of the elevated highway that lay straight north. I did not take that road but opted instead for Route 1A, an older route that hugged the coastline. This was a road that allowed the traveller to view the passing scenes within cozy, dimly-lit kitchens, to observe the knick-knacks on ice-tinged windowsills. As I walked I slid a tape into the machine listening to a band called The Police telling me that:

"There's a black hat caught in a high tree top
There's a flag pole rag and the wind won't stop"

On a curb near the city limit I watched the moon climb the frozen sky, bleeding its color into the air until it stood white, high, and sharply focused, adding its approval to the cold.

In the first car that stopped were two men going to the dog track in Revere. Talking of the ninth race, the driver's chin almost rested on the steering wheel as he promised, "They ain't foolin' this fool tonight."

The next ride was to downtown Salem where black witches adorned the copper flashing of ancient houses. Then came a tipsy fisherman who ran a bait shop in Newburyport, and who hated blue-fish, Jews, homosexuals, and the New York Yankees.

I stood in Newburyport for two hours, watching the couples in their foreign cars pass by, until a young man wearing a plaid hunting jacket, a beer in his hands, stopped. He was going to Nashua, New Hampshire, and he said. "I'm stoned, man, like you know, I can't hack it, and I'm really stoned, ya know?"

Unblinking, gripping the wheel as though he saw a road full of spiders, he brought us to Portsmouth, letting me off at the big traffic circle with a parting, "Sorry man, but I'm really wicked stoned."

I watched his car swing left and zoom off toward the hinterland of the Granite State.

For another hour I stood in the cold then went to a nearby Howard Johnson's for tea with lemon, and toast layered with cinnamon. I had a second cup of tea watching the waitresses in a wordless war, not meeting one another's gaze, slamming dishes, and ripping off receipts from their pads with tearing rage.

It was very late now and the next ride was from a trucker going to Bar Harbor for a shipment of lobster. He would rush through the night to make the turn-around in time for the next business day in Boston.

He dropped me off in Kennebunk where the stars in the eastern sky were losing part of their luminescence to a growing light there. The river was higher now, which made it seem less swift, and the cold was probing my clothes as were the thin branches of the genuflecting birch trees. A small animal scurried along the ground, quite brown and vulnerable in the snow as an owl sounded not far away.

As I walked I held the strap of the instruments and the walkman in one hand. They skimmed close to the crusted snow. The coming light began to define individual trees in such a subtle way that it seemed as though the ground itself was the source of the illumination.

A small brook, a familiar thicket, a stone wall, and the house came into view. One window held the pallid elongated moon, and the smoke from the woodstove rose and rose.

When I let myself in I was seized by a shiver, and it came again with even more force as I unlaced my boots in the kitchen. The boy was asleep, one arm over the blankets, and in the next room she lay beneath the greens and the reds of her afghan. She did not hear me undress at the foot of the bed. She did not stir as I stood for long minutes. The cold air mixed with the deep want as I watched her, finally knowing by the changed rhythm of her breathing that she was awake.

At length she rolled over, swallowing and drawing breaths deeper and deeper as I came to her, kissing her feet, her calves, the sides and backs of her knees, the deep softness of her thighs, her stomach, sides, breasts, her neck and her lips.

Outside, the light now seemed in retreat, and there was the sureness of the four walls, the deep softness of the mattress, and the musk and breathing of the woman. There was the hard unyielding want of my body and the cool air above us.

Then there was again the calling musk of her body, the salty depth of her mouth. There was this woman in my arms like the warm promise of life itself. There were all the other places and then the room, and then there was only the moist deep certainty of the woman.